TOCABAGA

THE TOCABAGA CHRONICLES

BOOK #1

THOMAS H.WARD

TOCABAGA

The Tocabaga Chronicles: Book #1

THOMAS H. WARD

Transcendent Publishing
PO Box 66202
St. Pete Beach, FL 33736
www.transcendentpublishing.com

ISBN-13: 978-0615894416

ISBN-10: 0615894410

Printed in the Unites States of America.

*"In every truth there is non-truth.
In every fiction there is non-fiction."*

—*Thomas H. Ward*

April 11, 2026

If you are reading this then you are one of the lucky ones or smart ones who have survived the first year of the collapse. I am writing these chronicles to pass on a history of what has happened, a history telling how we have survived so far. I do not reveal the full names of the people living here in case the Feds happen to come upon this. Read my story and tell others what has happened here. Pass it on; it may save your life.

My name is Jack Gunn and I live on Tocabaga. The real name will not be disclosed, nor the location. Tocabaga is a clue as to the general location of this island. It is a sanctuary where one can be safe from what is going on in the outside world. If you happen to come here, are of good character, and believe in the freedom of man and the Constitution, you are welcome to stay. The current population is 556 people. We help each other stay alive.

I am 63 years old and have traveled to forty countries in my lifetime. I have seen a lot of despair around the world, those poorer than poor with no hope of improving their lives. People are living in their own filth and stench, inside cardboard boxes without water that is safe to drink, or even a bathroom. Little kids pick through the garbage dumps for rotten food. It breaks my heart to see this. They have hyper-extended little bellies, which means they are starving to death. These people live day to day, meal to meal. They have no hope for a better life for them or their kids. What are we, what are you going to do about this?

It is so quiet here, so quiet I can hear the birds singing. You can hear the flutter of their wings and the wind blowing through the trees. There are no cars or noisy motors, no road noise at all. Every now and then you may hear a military plane fly overhead but not often.

It wasn't always like this. In the old days 5,000 cars would pass by my house on a holiday weekend going to the beach. The cars were loaded with people, grills, coolers, bikes, and boats. The peak time was the 4th of July weekend. Cars were bumper to bumper. July 4th Independence Day, what a great time we used to have going to the beach and watching the annual fireworks, as each year the city would try to make them bigger and better than the year before.

We used to have a 4th of July Parade and everyone decorated their cars with red, white, and blue paper streamers and followed the two fire trucks our city had, beeping their horns while driving, while we were waving American flags. Afterward we would all go to the only bar here for a drink with free hot dogs and burgers. We acted a little like hicks but it was fun for everyone. Boy, a hot dog with mustard and onions sure would taste great right now. We still celebrate July 4th with no parade and no hot dogs, but it means more to us now than it did a couple of years ago. Now we are really fighting to keep our freedom and Constitutional rights.

One thing we do hear are the sounds of drones flying overhead at night. They're like a buzzing bee, a low tone which you can barely discern. No one has ever seen a drone, we only hear them flying at night like bats. Drones have excellent night vision cameras and can identify any person. Drones can shoot missiles that have the ability to blow up a car or truck so the drones make everyone a little concerned. We know the government is watching us but why are they watching us?

Does someone think we are a threat to the country?

We are waiting for you to contact us by email to find where Tocabaga is located. There is an email address hidden within these chronicles.

I will reply.

THOMAS H. WARD

April 17, 2025

12 Months Earlier

My brother Ron, who was on guard duty, radioed me, "Ten cars are coming down the road, they must be the same ones the Rangers warned us about, so get your butts down here fast."

I radioed back, "Ron, we are on the way."

The rapid response team and all security persons grabbed their guns and headed to the bridge; a total of fifty men. No one said a word as we jumped into our vehicles but I knew everyone was worried about what would happen next. The sun was setting and soon it would be dark.

Ron spent 25 years in the Navy and was a Crew Chief. He retired as a Senior Chief Petty Officer. He made drug and illegal immigration arrests in the old days. The Crew Chief is the one who man's the 50-caliber guns and other small arms as well as makes any repairs needed during flight. He also was a chauffeur and bodyguard for an Atlantic Fleet Admiral and the Fleet's heavyweight boxing champion. Grandpa taught us how to box and shoot when we were kids. Grandpa used to box for money when he worked in the coal mines and he always carried a Colt .45 in his waistband. He was a tough old guy who died of a heart attack at the age of seventy-eight. He served in the Army in WWI and was in combat with the Russian Wolf Hounds. Ron is a great shooter and not afraid of anything. We're very close and I can trust him to do anything for me. Since the Civil War every man in my family has served in the Military.

Our compound is on an island with one way in and one way out over a two-lane guarded bridge. Our little island is a mile and a half wide and two miles long. This used to be a busy little place, with four restaurants, one bar, one church, one seven-eleven store, two gas stations, and two marinas. There are 1,975 housing units, which includes condos and homes. Once we had a little over 3,000 people living here, now it's reduced to the 556 remaining. I estimate there are about 1,200 abandoned cars and about 300 boats left by the people that used to live here. That means we have plenty of fuel and gasoline on hand.

When you leave the island your property becomes more or less community property. Cars, boats, houses and anything in the house such as food supplies, guns, or whatever, will be taken for the general good of the community. When you return, or if you return, you'll get your property back.

We have a lot of resources, materials, food, gas, guns and cars that are now targets for the criminals to steal. We have the resources and a location that is very desirable. We accept new people but we cannot let in any bad apples. The problem is finding out who is good and who is bad.

We all piled into our vehicles and drove as fast as

possible to the bridge, just three minutes away. Upon arriving, we saw Ron and my son Tommy standing behind a car watching the vehicles pull up to our roadblock. There were ten vehicles and I estimated at least forty people, who probably all had guns.

It looked like a scene right out of the old movie, "Mad Max," starring Mel Gibson. A bunch of beat-up old cars and evil-looking people inside them. I wondered how these jerks found our compound because it is not well known unless you are from around here and even then many locals do not know our location. The Mad Max cars stopped about 160 yards away.

I told Ron and Tommy, "Keep under cover while our other people get into position."

Everyone knew what to do as we had trained for this many times. Due to the uphill rise of the bridge our men were not visible to the potential enemy. They could only see about six people. My hands were sweating and my heart was racing. I was thinking, *What do these guys want? Whatever they want, it can't be good for us.*

Tommy spent eight years as a Marine Scout Sniper and fought in the Korean War in 2018, which only lasted sixty days. Thanks to him and other brave soldiers, Korea is now a united free country again. He received the Silver Star and is credited with 45 confirmed sniper kills. His weapon of choice is the Remington model 700, firing a Winchester .308 caliber bullet. He can hit a melon at 600 yards. He is the best long distance shooter we have. His real name is Thomas Matthew Gunn but he soon gained the nickname Tommy Gunn because of his shooting skill, named after the Thomson Submachine Gun called the "Tommy Gun."

Two men stepped forward holding a white flag and approached with no visible weapons and hands raised. Rick the duly elected head of our group, yelled to our men, "Everyone, hold your fire."

I told Ron and Tommy, "If these guys put their hands behind their backs, shoot them. They might have a gun hidden behind them."

Rick said, "Robbie and Jack put down your rifles. Let's go see what they want; we'll meet them halfway."

We still had our side arms on as we walked towards them. Like a shadow, Mark was following behind me carrying his pocket knife. Never take a knife to a gunfight is my motto but this was Mark's only weapon; he used it to skin fish.

We stopped walking and they came closer. I said, "That's close enough," putting them at about ten feet away.

We needed to keep some distance between us and these people in case a fight broke out. This would give us time to draw and shoot our handguns.

I looked at them, unshaven, in dirty clothes; they were grimy-looking people. I couldn't tell who they were but I didn't like the looks of them. My sixth sense was telling me these people weren't good apples.

The biggest guy asked, "Who is in charge?"

Rick replied, "I am, what do you want?"

You could feel the tension in the air. My eyes were fixed on these dirt bags; never ever take your eyes off the enemy. The wind blew their body odor in my direction and I almost gagged from the stench. They looked and smelled like they hadn't taken a shower in months. Their hair was long and both had long scraggly beards. They were just dirty-looking junkies. The type of people you want to avoid.

The larger guy said, "My name is Big Jim, what's your name?"

Big Jim was about 6'5" tall; the other guy was about my size at 5' 11" and 200 pounds. They both looked to be about forty years old but it was hard to tell.

Rick answered, "My name is not important, what do you want?"

Big Jim replied, "That's not very friendly of you. We are just good old boys from up north of here and we need food, guns, supplies, cars and gas. We are willing to trade. We have some women, slaves or drugs if you need any. We know you have the supplies we need, how about helping us out?"

That was our clue that these were very dangerous men. I felt sorry for the women being used as slaves.

Rick answered, "We have nothing for you. We cannot spare anything and we don't need any slaves or women."

Big Jim looked at the other guy and whispered something in his ear, then said, "You must need something, let's make a deal. Look at how many men I got, we can take anything we want from your little group but we don't want any trouble. We just want to come in and look around, take what we want and leave."

I wanted these guys dead for making that threat.

You could tell they were big dope-heads and meth users. Half their teeth were missing. I kept staring at this Big Jim; he looked familiar but I couldn't remember from where. His huge head, the Neanderthal shape of it, or size of it, was different. I was thinking, *Where have I seen him before?*

I asked, "How many slaves do you have? Let us see them and maybe we can make a deal."

Big Jim replied, "We got five."

Big Jim told the man next to him to get the slaves. While they were walking back, I saw one woman about 25 years old, two young boys about 12 years old and two young girls about 10 to 12 years old. They were tied up with ropes around their hands and necks.

Robbie and Rick both looked at me and Rick leaned over and whispered in my ear, "What are you doing?"

I just whispered back in his ear as soft as possible, "Trust me and follow my lead."

The slaves were standing next to Big Jim with their heads hanging down and they looked in terrible shape. I felt anger and sorrow at the same time.

I took off my gold chain necklace and said, "I'll trade you this 18K gold chain for all five slaves. It is worth about $20,000 on the market."

My wife purchased the chain for me on our 20th wedding anniversary so it had great meaning and value to me.

Jim said, "Let me see it."

I stepped forward to hand it over to him, he reached out and grabbed it from my hand very quickly as if to say, give me that you fool. I didn't even like the idea of him touching my chain.

He looked closely at the chain and verified it was 18K and then he said, "That's not enough for all five. I need more than this but I'll keep it as a down payment until we reach a deal." He stuffed the chain into his front pocket.

Big Jim just made a big-ass mistake. That really pissed me off and I looked right into his eyes. He knew I was mad and I could see a smirk on his face, he liked what he was doing. He was a bully and I hate bullies. He was use to getting his way by intimidation because of his size but that didn't scare me as I knew I could kill him in an instant.

I had no intention of letting him keep my gold chain.

Then it hit me. I knew who this Big Jim was, I saw him about a year ago while I was peering through my rifle scope in the dark. I saw his silhouette, which was frozen in my memory, the shape of the head, the size of his huge Neanderthal head, and his beard rang a bell.

I had enough of this talk and knew I had to kill these two guys. I looked at Robbie, I looked at Rick; he didn't know what to do now or what say to these slimy dirt bags. I was thinking that talking time was over. I hoped Tommy had his 308 aimed at these jerks.

The clock was ticking; I could feel they were going to make a move.

THOMAS H. WARD

April 11, 2025

6 Days Earlier

We heard the helicopters coming before we saw them. Security ran out into the street, guns ready, to see who dared to fly over our island. To our surprise they were Army Black Hawk helicopters, which relieved our fears so we didn't shoot at them. We had never seen Army choppers over our island. They flew by, circled around, and then came back lower than before.

The four Black Hawk UH 60 choppers hovered at about one hundred feet in the air and started to land in the street, creating a whirlwind of dust. The people who gathered there to watch them land backed up a few hundred feet to get out of the way. We were all surprised and wondered what they wanted. As far as we were concerned the Army was on our side.

The Black Hawk helicopter is armored to withstand hits from 23 mm shells, and its airframe is designed to crush on impact to protect the crew. The pilot and co-pilot have armor plated seats. The helicopter also accommodates door gunners, who provide security for the crew and aircraft using machine guns.

Upon landing, eight Army Rangers jumped out from each chopper in full battle gear, pointing their guns at the crowd that had gathered. Everyone, including me, started to back up and give them space; most of us with guns raised our hands to show we meant them no harm. I was thinking, *what the hell is going on. Why are they pointing their guns at us?*

The Ranger motto is, "Rangers Lead the Way." They are tough as nails. This was the first visit by the Army and we wanted news from the outside world to learn what was occurring out there. We had heard over the radio that the Army Special Forces were now involved fighting for the common American citizen.

As the chopper motors wound down and the noise reduced, a Ranger Captain approached us and asked, "Who is in charge?"

I was standing there with Rick, Robbie and Eddy. I stepped forward and said, "We are in charge Captain and you are a welcome sight. What can we do for you?"

The Captain replied, "First of all, please instruct your people not to point any guns towards my men. Keep all rifles slung over your shoulder and handguns holstered as we don't want any accidents to happen."

I yelled out his instructions for everyone to hear as I did not want any accident to happen either. Rick, Robbie and Eddy walked around the crowd making sure everyone complied with this order.

After a few minutes the Captain seemed satisfied as our people laid down their guns or slung them over their shoulders and he said, "We heard about your little compound and since we were flying by on our way south; I decided to drop in to find out more about this location and the people living here."

I said, "Captain, may I suggest we go inside in the shade and talk?"

The Captain told his men to stand down and they stopped pointing their weapons at us. They still stood there on each side of the choppers, watching everyone, guns at the ready.

Four of us, along with the Ranger Captain and one Ranger Master Sergeant, went into what was once the local bar.

After proper introductions and handshakes, Captain Sessions said, "Rick, please tell me a little about this island compound, what laws you follow, how many people live here and how it generally functions."

Rick said, "We are all property owners living here and I am the President and Jack is Vice President and Director of Security for our compound. We are governed by the state and county laws and for law enforcement, we fall under the County Sheriff Office. Twenty-five of us are Sheriff Deputies. We follow the US Constitution and Bill of Rights. We have a Board of Directors that is elected by the people living here.

"There are twenty-five military veterans on our island, Marines, Navy, and Air Force but most are Army vets. Most vets were only in the military for four years but they know how to follow orders. Three of our men are retired from the military; Ron a retired Navy Chief Petty Officer, Bob a retired Marine; and Mike retired from the Army. Their knowledge and combat skills are helpful to everyone. Tommy Gunn was a Marine Scout Sniper and won the Silver Star. They drilled our security team into shape and set the rules of conduct and rules for engagement with any possible enemy."

We held a vote for President of our compound and Rick won. Not many wanted that job. Everyone likes Rick and he has a certain way of making you listen to him. Maybe it is his deep voice and reasonable logic. Rick has a brother who is an FBI agent but he hasn't seen him for years. Rick is a self-made millionaire who used to own a tow truck company. He has no military experience.

I was elected Vice President and Director of Security because no one else wanted the job and maybe because I had the most experience. I had actually killed more people than anyone else, other than my son.

I have had many different jobs in my life. I spent four years in the Army as a Military Policeman. I have been trained to use handguns, rifles, and shotguns, and in hand-to-hand combat. I once worked for a government Contractor in Security and had a DOD (Department of Defense) secret clearance and AEC (Atomic Energy Commission) security clearance.

I obtained a degree in Engineering, but I never lost my fondness for guns and shooting. I joined gun clubs and shot in the IDPA for ten years. The International Defense Pistol League or IDPA has you practice drawing and shooting once or twice a week. You become a very fast draw and a very accurate shooter. I was also a range officer for ten years. I would go shooting with many friends, some of whom were retired Navy Seals, Army Rangers, Marines, DEA Agents and Police Officers. I shot with some of the best shooters in the area. One thing I know about is guns. I have shot almost every type of gun made at one time or another. Not only do l know how to use them, I know how to fix most of them and can sight in rifles with or without scopes.

My main job here is teaching people how to shoot and clean their weapons. I want everyone to know how to use a gun. In addition I pull security duty when it is my turn. Since I know something about security, I helped set up our security system for the compound.

I once shot a taxi driver in Mexico who tried to rob me. It was 5 am and I was in a taxi going to the Mexico City airport, when the taxi driver decided to take me down some dark road and rob me of my money. He stopped the car in the middle of nowhere, got out, and pulled a gun, commanding me, "Get out, Senor," which I did.

As I stood there within reach of his gun, he ordered me, "Give me your money and wallet."

I said, "Sure, just don't shoot me."

As I pulled my money out of my pocket, I dropped it on the ground and his eyes looked down at it, giving me a split second to use a trick I learned from a Navy Seal, which is how to disarm and kill someone within your reach. As I grabbed and twisted the gun barrel it fired, the bullet hit his head and I pulled the gun from his hand and fired two more times into his chest.

He was dead. I said to myself, maybe out loud but I don't recall, "See you just killed yourself, you fucking dummy!"

I looked around to see if anyone else was nearby, but since gun fire in Mexico City is a common sound, no one paid any attention. In addition, most people don't want to get involved.

I used to practice this disarm move all the time with Robbie and my buddies at our fight club and it was drummed into my muscle memory. Once you make the move you have to complete it or you will get shot. You swat the inside of the gun hand at his wrist while at the same time grab the gun barrel, turning it in and up towards the gunman's head. Of course the gunman is going to pull the trigger but muscle reflex reaction time is not fast enough and by the time he pulls the trigger the gun barrel is pointed at his own head. Bam, he shoots himself in the head, it works almost every time. You carry through by twisting the gun out of his hand, which breaks his finger because it is in the trigger guard, and the gun falls into your hand; while stepping back, you shoot him again to make sure he is dead, just in case the head bullet missed.

I wiped off all fingerprints in the taxi and from the gun, throwing the gun on the ground next to his hand. I took off his white gloves that all the taxi drivers wore in Mexico and put them on. Now I looked just like a cab driver. I jumped into the taxi and sped away, leaving his dead body lying on the side of the road, and drove myself to the airport, pulling up right in front at the drop-off zone. To my surprise a Mexican cop was standing there looking right at me.

I grabbed my bag from the back seat and walked inside to the ticket counter, leaving the cab sitting there, without making eye contact with the cop. I watched the cop out of the corner of my eye, as he was walking away, paying no attention to the cab. He thought I was just another poor cab driver. It was a good thing I had on those white gloves, jeans, and a ball cap. As the plane rose into the air I thanked God I made it out of Mexico. I never felt any remorse for killing that jerk because he most likely would have killed me.

Rick and I own a lot of guns. We have collected guns and ammo for over 25 years because we like guns and always thought of them as the best item to own in a crisis. No question, a gun is the one item to own. Think about it, if you have a gun you can protect your family and hunt food. One time Rick asked me if he should buy some gold for emergency situations and future worth. I told him no, buy guns and ammo. If you don't have a gun then someone can take your gold. I once heard there are three hundred-fifty million guns in the United States, which means one gun for every man, woman and child living in the good old USA.

Between Rick and I we have 55 guns; you name it, we own it. We have shotguns, AR15 rifles, AK47 rifles, a Cobb 50 caliber long range rifle, 308 sniper rifles, HK 93 and HK 92 battle rifles and all kinds of handguns. Most handguns are 9mm along with some .380, .357 and .45 ACP colts. We have a lot of ammunition for each gun and can do reloading of spent shells. At our location we have a total of 465 guns, almost one gun per person.

I carry at all times a Glock 17, 9mm with 3 mags and a Colt AR15 carbine 9 mm with a red dot low light scope along with three 30-round mags in a leg pouch strapped to my left leg. In addition, I carry a double-edge Black Bear Bowie knife. You never know when a good knife will come in handy. Ever since I stabbed the junkie who broke into my house, I've always carried some type of knife. I keep my Glock in a Kydex plastic holster on my right hip. The plastic holster keeps the gun secure, allows for easy access and a fast draw. Every security person here carries a gun at all times as you never know when you may need one.

Captain Sessions said, "That is what I wanted to hear, you follow the US Constitution and Bill of Rights, along with local laws. You are not an outlaw band keeping people here against their will."

I said, "We can assure you everyone is here of their own free will. Go around and talk to anyone you like. The people living here can leave anytime they want. Most of the people that previously lived here have already left to go live in the green zones, leaving us with a total of 556 people in our compound."

Sessions replied, "We're already interviewing your people while we are sitting here to check out your story."

I thought this guy was smart. He had a plan all along.

We all started to laugh. Robbie raised his beer and said, "A toast to freedom and the Constitution."

Everyone clinked their glasses together and said, "To freedom and the Constitution."

We had no sooner made a toast and in the door came a Ranger who advised the Captain that they had talked to twenty people who all stated they were here of their own free will. It felt great to gain the Rangers' trust.

The Captain replied, "Good then, we have confirmed your story, now let's see your compound. First tell me about any problems and dangers you may have here."

I replied, "Captain, here is the situation. Empty homes are being taken back by the jungle. Grass and weeds have grown so high that you cannot walk through them without fear of getting bit by a snake. We have a large number of rattlesnakes for some reason. I killed two of them on my patio the other day. Every day I see at least one snake."

Robbie butted in, which he does all the time, "Sometimes the electric power comes on for a few hours a day but not enough to cool a house. We are blacked out for hours at a time. You never know when or for how long the power will be on. That means no electric lights at night and everything is black. At night it gets really dark and this is when snakes come out to hunt so not many people move around at night. If you walk around at night you need to stay on the sidewalks and roadways.

"There are a few generators which we use for running a small air conditioner, charging cell phones and tablets. Yes, we have cell phone service every now and then and are able to access the internet for news. What we see and hear is not good. We can also charge our phones using car plugs. We made some windmills and solar cells to generate 12 volts of power to run 12-volt lights and fans. A small fan can reduce the heat index by about 10 degrees, which makes a difference. Almost everyone has a fan."

Rick commented, "We are lucky to get water from the city water supply so we can take showers, but only with cold water only because there's no electric power. However, we can use the toilets. Thank God for that benefit. Keeping clean is important to stay healthy. You need good sanitary conditions to keep disease from taking hold. We boil all water before drinking it as no one can be sure if it is totally safe. The big problem for us is having enough soap. Soap is not easy to make and we don't have lye or animal fat to produce it. We can only obtain it when we go to town to trade or barter for goods and food."

Eddy who worries about the little things like bugs, jumped in with his concerns saying, "There are killer bees here and they are extremely dangerous so we try to stay away from them. The only thing you can do is burn the nest if you can find it but who is brave enough to do that? Nasty little bugs I hate them all. So far only a few people have been stung with no serious reactions.

"We are infected with Black Widows and Recluse spiders, which are two of the most dangerous types. Black Widows have been here as long as I can remember. They make thick sticky webs and eat anything. I have never been bit by one but others here have. To treat the bite you need antibiotics. The female spider is very big and usually has a red hourglass spot on the stomach. The Brown Recluse is very dangerous and I have been bitten twice. If you don't treat this bite it will rot your skin away in the bite area and possibly kill you. Needless to say, I hate spiders."

Sessions said, "Well, sounds pretty much normal, anything else?"

I replied, "My concern is not the bugs, snakes or spiders but the dangerous people who will kill you and your family for a can of beans, guns, gold, car or anything that suits their fancy. These dangerous people are the gangs, terrorists and criminals running loose causing our society to fall into disarray. I guess that's it."

Sessions started to laugh and said, "Well, that is quite a list, and I agree with you, dangerous people are the main concern for us also. Now can we review your defensive positions for the compound?"

Sessions wanted to ascertain our methods for

protecting our compound and find out how we obtained food. We showed them our first line of defense, the one and only road into our compound. He was impressed that we had cars interlocked blocking the road so no one could just drive through and also liked the fact that 24/7 we had sixteen people on guard.

Captain Sessions asked me, "What type of weapons do you have and how many?"

I said, "We have a lot of weapons, mostly handguns and rifles, nothing big but a Cobb 50; I'll give you a list."

I provided him with a list of every weapon we had and to whom it was issued. The list also kept track of the ammunition, which was all stored at what use to be the local bank. The bank is our armory and it is under guard at all times.

I advised Sessions, "All weapon cleaning is performed by the person each gun is issued too and any repair work needed is performed by myself, Bob, Mike and Tommy."

Captain Sessions commented, "There is not much I can do to improve what you have already done but do you have a fallback plan with another defensive position?"

Robbie advised, "No, not really, our idea is to hold that entrance at all cost. We have a total of about 96 security people. That is the choke point; if the bad guys get near us there, then we have a problem."

Sessions replied, "I suggest you redo the bridge controls so you can control it from this side of the channel. Once the bridge is opened up no one can cross."

We all agreed that was a good idea but doing it was another problem, I didn't know if we had the technology to do so. That was something I'd have to check on.

Sessions inquired, "What do you need in the way of supplies, food or water?"

I said, "We are in pretty good shape for food and water. What we need is ammo, bulletproof vests and most of all medical supplies. In addition we need bug spray, hand soap and laundry soap."

Captain Sessions, while taking notes, advised us that Special Operations was now involved in local fighting, trying to bring law and order back to the country.

This is a good thing and maybe it will make life better. Maybe there is hope that things will turn around and be brighter in the future, I thought.

Sessions finally asked, "Are you willing to take in some new people?"

"Like who and how many?" Rick asked.

The Captain admitted to us that things were not getting better any time soon and some of his men had family that they wanted to protect.

Sessions said, "We want to bring Ranger families here."

Rick replied, "Yes, we welcome them; we have enough food and supplies. It is the least we can do to show support to our troops."

Stores run out of food all the time. Trucks carrying food are robbed and the goods are sold on the black market. No truck is safe on the open highway. Farmers cannot get their goods to the food processing centers and those food companies cannot get the food to the stores. No person is safe unless you travel in a convoy and are armed to the teeth.

Schools have shut down except in the green zone in the inner city. Most kids are home schooled now as it is safer. Kids on a school bus are easy targets for kidnapping.

The government is now controlling the food and there are food lines at every store. You must wait for hours to get anything. If you can find and buy staples, they are only enough for a few days. You cannot feed your family on a loaf of bread. Fresh vegetables and fruit are not available. Supplies are reduced to canned goods or freeze-dried, ready-to-eat meals, same as the Army rations.

Captain Sessions replied, "That's great, it's a big relief for me and my men. We plan to bring in about 200 people, mostly women and older kids, and some retired Rangers, if that is ok. We also plan to use the empty island south of here as a Ranger base of operations in this area."

Eddy said, "You mean No Man's Land? That's what we call it. How many Rangers will be based there?"

Sessions replied, "There will be about five hundred men."

I advised, "We guard the bridge leading to it, and use that area for raising chickens and growing most of our produce. It would be great to have a base there."

Sessions answered, "Yes, we know a lot about your group as our drones have been watching you."

Rick commented, "We wondered who was sending the drones to spy on us." We all laughed, relieved that now we knew the reason for the drones.

Captain Sessions said, "Well, that about wraps up our meeting. We'll be back in a few days."

Eddy, who would give you the shirt off his back, commented to the Captain, "It is our honor to be of service."

By the time we got back to the choppers his men were sitting around talking to our people and seeming to get along quite well. It looked like one big happy family and I noticed our people had given the Rangers drinks and snacks to enjoy.

Sessions went over to one chopper, took out a box of grenades and gave them to me.

That was great, as we had no such explosive devices other than Molotov cocktails. These are glass bottles filled with gasoline and a rag stuffed in the top. You light it and throw it as hard as you can …BOOM… it is a big fire bomb when the glass bottle breaks. The problem is these are dangerous to store and handle. So we don't keep them on hand but can make them quickly if needed.

Captain Sessions said, "We will bring more bulletproof vests, grenades and maybe other little goodies with us when we come back. By the way, coming here we saw ten cars about 60 miles away heading this direction. We don't know if they are friend or foe, so be careful. See you soon."

He told his Rangers to mount up. They all boarded the Black Hawk UH 60 choppers. The motors started to whine, the big blades turning slowly at first and then gaining speed until they were only a blur. They lifted off one at a time, leaving in a whirlwind of dust. About 200 people watched the Rangers leave and goofy as it sounds, we all waved goodbye.

The Rangers visit let us know we were no longer on our own and could depend on them for help and supplies. It gave us all a feeling of security, one we hadn't had in a long time.

Now we were waiting for the Rangers to come back. It had been five days. *Where were they?*

THOMAS H. WARD

May 13, 2024

11 Months Earlier

*A*t this time U. S. unemployment had reached a whopping 55 percent and inflation was at 28% a year. There were a lot of cheap homes available if you had the money to pay cash. Gasoline skyrocketed to around $25.00 per gallon if you could find it. Many people out of work were roaming the streets looking for handouts, food or some kind of work. Things were out of control and every month the unemployment numbers went up another point. Finally, the government stopped the news media from putting out the unemployment percentages and inflation rate.

Everyone could see the prices going up each week. Fifty out of every 100 people did not have a job. Every day I heard about someone who lost their job. Things were getting worse every day, every month but everyone thought the economy would get better because the President told us the worst was over.

Maybe you can remember the attack at the Boston Marathon back in 2013, or the other random attacks committed by radical Islamists. These terrorist acts were becoming normal, along with other violence committed by skinheads and gangs. We needed to carry a gun everywhere we went for protection against people who would kill for a car, money or food.

For us it all started one summer night about 4 am. This is when we realized how bad things were becoming. I was woken up in the middle of the night by gunfire. I listened carefully to determine the type of gun used and the location. You can tell the type of gun by the sound it makes when it is fired. These were AK47 rifles, the preferred guns of gangs, cartels, and terrorists because they were cheap.

An AK 47 fires a 7.62 x 39mm round. It is an assault rifle developed in the old Soviet Union by Mikhail Kalashnikov in 1947. Officially it is called the Auto Kalashnikov hence AK 47. It is the weapon of choice for terrorists since it is cheap and readily available. Worldwide more of these guns were produced than any other type. It is a sturdy rifle and dangerous at close range but it is not very accurate.

Pulling on my pants, I grabbed my Glock 9mm and stuffed it into my waistband. I went to my gun safe and pulled out my Colt AR 15 9mm carbine along with 3 mags of ammunition. After picking up my cell phone, I ran out the door.

The AR 15 rifle is a lightweight, 5.56 mm/.223-caliber, magazine-fed, air cooled rifle. It is manufactured with extensive use of aluminum alloys and synthetic materials. The AR 15 was first built by Arma Lite, hence the meaning of AR, a small arms manufacture. They sold the design to Colt Firearms. Colt redsigned the rifle and Government renamed it the

M16. Colt then started selling the semi-automatic version of the M16 rifle as the Colt AR-15 for civilian sales. The AR 15 H barrel is identical to the M16 the only difference being the AR 15 is only sold in semi-automatic. There many types of AR designed rifles and carbines. Orginally CAR was meant to mean Colt Automatic Rifle but with shorter barrels becoming popular it now means carbine model which means the barrel is shorter than the standard rifle. The AR can also be purchased to fire .22L, 9 mm pistol ammunition or larger rounds.

My phone rang. It was my son Tommy, who asked, "What's going on?"

I said, "Meet me outside with your rifle, there is gunfire coming from the local 7-11 down the street."

The 7-11 was open 24 hours a day. Looking down the street I saw the Sheriff's car with its flashing lights on, sitting in the middle of the street. The Deputy was standing behind his car firing his handgun; I could see the flashes of fire coming from the barrel.

All of a sudden I heard footsteps behind me. I turned to fire and saw it was my neighbor Steve who had an M-14 rifle in his hand.

The M-14 rifle fires a 7.62x51mm NATO round and it was the main battle rifle for the Army until it was replace by the M 16.

Steve said, "What the hell is going on?"

I said, "Steve, you scared the shit out of me, I

almost shot you."

Steve scared me, but I was glad to see him. Soon my son showed up, meeting us in the middle of the divided highway under the cover of thick bushes. We slowly approached and saw the Sheriff Deputy fall down in the street.

Tommy said, "Look at that! The Deputy just got shot, what should we do?"

I replied, "Nothing right now, there are too many of them."

"I can shoot some of them from here and they won't know where the shot came from," Tommy replied.

"Wait; don't shoot unless they come closer."

Steve agreed.

I saw four cars and with about sixteen men ransacking the store, as I looked through my rifle scope. One big dude walked over to the officer and shot him again, then he took the cop's handgun. I could not make out his face, only his silhouette, but his big dark evil shape and huge head with a big beard was burned into my brain.

About ten minutes went by and the flashing lights of more Sheriffs' cars were coming over the one and only bridge that let people on and off our island. There were only three vehicles, which meant a total of three officers. They had no chance against a gang of sixteen men.

The gang members just stood on the side of the road and started shooting at the police. The three cars ran the gauntlet of gunfire and were heading towards us about 500 yards away. They slammed on the brakes, screeching to a stop near our location and the Deputies jumped out.

As they hid behind their cars one officer, Deputy Matthews, saw us after we called out to him; he knew us since he lives on the island, and told the other two officers, "Stand down, these are my friends."

We ran over to Matthews's car and ducked down. The rifle fire had stopped for now.

Matthews asked, "What the hell is going on?"

I said, "It seems some guys are robbing the store and I think they killed the Deputy."

Matthews got on his radio and called for more backup. Amazingly, the officers were not wounded from the gunfire when they came over the bridge but their cars where shot up. Lucky for them the bad guys were crummy shots.

Looking down the street, we were surprised to see the gangs' cars pull out over the bridge, one by one leaving the island, randomly shooting their guns at us as they left.

The big dude who shot the Deputy stood in the street and shouted, "We'll be back." He aimed his rifle at us and fired off a couple of rounds that pinged off a police cruiser as we ducked for cover. His car, the last to leave sped away burning rubber.

The Deputies jumped in their cars and went to the aid of the fallen officer. I asked my son to take our rifles back to the house, just to be safe, as I didn't want them in our hands when more police backup arrived. I didn't want to get shot by mistake.

Steve and I ran to the store only to find a bloody mess. They left one dead officer, two dead store clerks and one dead bridge attendant. That explained why the bridge was not raised. Whenever a robbery is committed here the Deputy calls the bridge attendant to raise the bridge so they cannot escape the island. The gang must have shot the bridge attendant first.

This was our first encounter with gang attacks on our island. About 30 minutes later the Sheriff himself showed up with about a 15-man Swat Team that roped off the area. By that time it was almost daylight and most people who lived near the store were out in the street wondering what had happened.

The Sheriff roped off the area with yellow tape. Everyone stood around gawking while the coroner came and took the bodies away after the crime scene was searched for evidence. Officers were asking everyone there to come forward if they saw anything.

I advised them that all I saw were the four black cars and I didn't know the makes. I also saw the officer get shot but I didn't see the shooter's face; it was too dark and I could only see shapes. There was not much evidence. The spent shells on the ground were collected to see if they could be traced and would be held for future evidence in case they caught one of the scum bags with the gun that matched the shells. Chances are they would never be caught.

We called an emergency meeting with the Sheriff about providing more protection than one officer round the clock. Deputy Matthews commented that since he lived on the island, he could be stationed there 24-7 to provide protection but he still needed three more Deputies. The Sheriff agreed as this solved his problem and ours without costing him any more officers.

I said, "Why not swear in any man that wants to be

a Deputy who has some military training?"

The Sherriff agreed to this as long as Matthews was left in charge and we all reported to him. Twenty-four men stepped forward to take the oath. The problem was solved, for the time being. That night eight men were on duty guarding the bridge. Everyone slept well that night except me.

The County Sheriff recommended that we all move to the new green zone or the so-called protected zone downtown in the city, as he could no longer offer us protection. This was not for me as two or three families were crammed into one small room. You lived where they told you to live. Oddly enough, that day about 1500 people moved to the green zone, leaving their homes as well as extra cars, as you were only permitted to have one car in the green zone, due to parking problems. The next day another 944 people left leaving about 556 who wanted to stay in their homes.

I thought fine, let them go, as they would be a burden on the people who had the guts to stay and fight to protect their homes and lifestyle. No one was going to kick me out of my home. Now I was lucky as my two kids, son-in-law, daughter-in-law, granddaughter and brother lived on the island with my wife and I. We were all excellent shooters and long ago I started buying guns and ammunition. Most of the people that stayed also had guns and knew how to use them. I had drawn up a defensive plan years ago with my friend Eddy, a plan to protect our island from looting after a hurricane.

We decided to call a meeting the next day to elect officers for our new security organization and to discuss the subject of how we would protect our homes, as well as other civil matters. It was time for us to get serious about self defense, time to become serious about defending our homes, family and our American way of life. We had heard about these gangs and terrorist attacks but never seen one. Now attacks were becoming common all over the city. The police could do nothing about this as there were too many bad guys and too few officers.

The first directive was to guard and protect our location, 24 hours per day, seven days a week. We needed a total of 16 men for each eight-hour shift. This meant a grand total of 48 people to cover us around the clock. But we also needed time off as we couldn't work seven days a week, so we had to recruit 48 more people to cover the weekends two days a week. They would also act as rapid response team members. This brought the total number of people for security to ninety-six. Ninety-six people are a considerable force to protect our location, but necessary to defeat anyone who would do us harm.

This left 460 people to work on other necessary projects for our island such as fishing, farming, cooking, cutting grass, cutting trees and garbage pickup. Everyone would be assigned a job and no one would get a free ride.

I knew the gang would be back sooner or later. They always come back.

April 17, 2025

Continued

Suddenly Big Jim made a movement with his right hand, reaching around to his back. In an instant I drew my Glock 9mm out from its Kydex holster… Bam! Bam! Bam! I shot Big Jim with a triple tap, which is one bullet in the head and two in the chest. Big Jim never knew what hit him.

A Glock is without a doubt the best hand gun ever made. The barrels never wear out and they are very dependable. It will fire under water, you can throw it in the mud or run it over with a truck, and it still works every time. It is light weight and has a 15 to 17 round magazine capacity, which means you can fire a lot of bullets. I like the luger 9mm round because it is the most common hand gun ammunition. It is used by the military and police departments all over the United States.

At almost the same time, Robbie and I shot the other guy twice in the chest. They were dead; they both fell like a lead sinker, hitting the pavement with a thud.

The slaves fell to the ground begging us not to shoot them.

Ricked yelled, "What the hell are you guys doing shooting someone under a white flag?"

I yelled back, "Rick, I had no time to tell you or Robbie, but these are the guys who shot the Deputy a year ago at the 7-11 store. I recognized the big dork from that night."

A dork is defined as a whale penis; another meaning is a big prick.

I walked over to his body and found a gun behind his back tucked into the waistband. Just as I thought it was a Glock 9mm, which is standard police issue. I took my gold chain out of his dirty pocket, wiped it off, and slipped it back over my head.

I said, "Look here is the gun that the dork took off the cop."

Robbie checked the other guy and found another Glock. Most gang members don't carry an expensive Glock; they usually have a cheap old .38 special revolver, what we call a midnight special, a hot gun sold illegally. Later Deputy Matthews checked the serial numbers and they were police-issued; one belonged to Deputy Hardy, who was killed that terrible night a year ago.

I told Robbie, "Good shooting, Bro, I knew you would start shooting when I did."

Then I ordered, "Mark feed these guys to the sharks and hurry up!" Mark, strong as an ox, picked them up and tossed them over the bridge railing into the shark-infested water.

Mark laughed while saying, "You fucks are fish food; you don't mess with Jack Gunn."

As I was moving to a safe spot behind a car I ordered, "Take cover and make your way back up the bridge before we get shot!"

Robbie, Rick and I had the slaves in tow, pulling them along with us as well as we could. They were in shock. Eddy laying low, came up and took the slaves out of the range of fire back over the bridge. They would be safe and in good hands now.

Robbie, one of my best friends whom I have known more than 20 years, used to love to fight. I guess it was to prove his manhood. We used to have a fight club that would meet every month and we would practice the skills of self defense. We had six people in our club, one was a Navy Seal and another was a retired DEA agent. Back then Robbie did not own any guns for fear he would kill someone due to his quick temper. Many times I was with him and he would start a fight with someone for no reason at all. If a man looked at him wrong Robbie would just walk up and sucker-punch him.

Rick was still bitching about me shooting the dork, and I told him, "Look, there was nothing else I could do. He was wanted for killing a cop and they threatened to attack us. I figured if we shot the assholes then the rest of them wouldn't mess with us."

Rick is a good guy but he thinks too much and is slow to react. He said, "You can't shoot people in cold blood."

I answered back, "Look, I knew those guys had

guns and they were making a move. We were going to fight them anyway, no matter how you look at it, so drop it. We also saved five people from hell."

Robbie told Rick, "Shut the fuck up Bro, it's over, we're alive and they're fish food."

Mark exclaimed, "Yeah, fish food!"

Mark is a guy who does what he wants, when he wants. He does not like authority. Mark is single and yes Mark is a little crazy, so most people here stay away from him. Deep down however, Mark is a good guy who would do anything for me because I pay attention to him. I think he considers me a father figure since his own has passed away. One drawback is Mark likes to smoke pot.

A story from years ago is Mark had just purchased a new truck and drove downtown to buy pot. Well, the police had a sting set up and started chasing him in his truck. Mark tried to get away but the police stopped him.

The Officer asked him, "Why are you running from us?"

Mark replied, "Because you're chasing me."

The police asked him for his license and Mark said, "It's on the back of the truck."

Now who gives answers like that to the police? They found the pot in his truck. He was arrested for the dope and was also charged with fleeing and eluding the police. He spent eight months in jail and they took his truck for running drugs. Now Mark rides a bicycle everywhere. Mark works as a handyman, so if you need something done, Mark will do it. All-in-all, Mark just wants someone to notice him. But never call him crazy to his face.

Rick had never killed anyone and always wanted to give the other person the benefit of the doubt. I saw him get beat up pretty bad in a bar fight once because of that. My thinking is, shoot first and ask questions later. When in doubt, let God sort it out. This is the Wild West, where you shoot the other guy first or you die. Here there is no such thing as a fair fight.

I think the gang was in shock seeing their two big leaders blown away and thrown into the water like fish food because it took them about ten minutes to react. As we were taking cover, all of a sudden we heard a shot fired and we ducked behind a car. We didn't see where it came from but our men were returning fire at the gang below. Fifty guns firing all in a space of a few minutes are loud as hell. I saw a couple of dirt bags fall as the dummies were standing out in the open shooting at us. It seemed they had no training at all. After three more scumbags fell, they ran behind their trucks and cars.

I guessed that Tommy had shot at least three of these jerks. Now they were taking pot shots at us but their aim was so bad the bullets just whizzed overhead or hit the cars around us. The gang started to jump in their vehicles to make a getaway. Our fire power was overwhelming. They didn't expect that.

I yelled to our people, "Hold your fire, save your ammo!"

The gang withdrew, driving down the road about a mile to the empty condos abandoned two years ago. My guess is more than a few were also wounded by our excellent shooters.

I told Mark, "Go down there and dump the bodies in the water. Robbie, go with him and make sure they are all dead."

Rick and I watched as Robbie put a bullet in the head of each of the bodies. Rick and I looked at each other and started to laugh at what Robbie just did, but we were laughing in relief that we won this round with none of us hurt. Mark and Robbie carried back three AK47 rifles and a few mags.

Just north of us, about a mile away, there used to be a big condo and townhome community. Now it is empty, for the most part, and falling apart. Homeless people, gangs, criminals, terrorists, and other dangerous people have taken it over. They would like to take over our island and homes but we won't let that happen. Some in small groups of five or six have already tried to come here over the bridge or gain access by boat. They all died trying so they don't try any more.

After the battle, most of us went down to the bar for a beer and a lot of people gathered around us and wanted to know what had happened. Everyone was worried but they were all happy we weren't hurt. I hate having to tell a story over and over again, but Mark likes to tell stories so we all just let him tell it in his own way, which can be quite funny most of the time, but not always accurate.

The slaves were checked out by Doc Scott at our clinic to see if they needed medical assistance. Doc said they just needed food and water. Several families who had no kids stepped up to the plate and volunteered to take them in, including the older woman. They are all in good hands now.

We could hear gunfire coming from the condo area and guessed that the same gang that was just here was engaging with the criminals now living in the condos. With any luck they would kill each other off. It was dark now and we wondered what would happen next.

What will we do tomorrow?

THOMAS H. WARD

April 18, 2025

L ast night nothing happened except we heard continuous sporadic gunfire. We left ten people on guard at the bridge, figuring that would be enough until others could arrive. I don't think anyone slept well, worrying about what would happen the next day. I dozed off a few times, getting about an hour of sleep. My whole family slept together that night. We took turns serving a two-hour guard duty just in case.

Ron, Tommy, Robbie and I drove down to the bridge around 7 am after a great fried fish and orange juice breakfast. Rick was there, it seems he spent the night on guard duty.

I asked Rick, "Anything new?"

Rick replied, "Nothing, you can only hear gunfire every now and then. Jack, I am sorry about yesterday; you were right and I will back you up that they were making a move for their guns."

I stated, "I don't think anyone is going to put me in jail for killing two bad guys, so forget about it." I think Rick chose to pull guard duty all night because he was sorry for chewing us out over killing the two dorks.

I suggested, "Rick, let's have a meeting to decide what we'll do next. We can't let a force of thirty armed people control our one and only way out of here for very long."

Rick asked, "Who do you think should attend the meeting?"

Eddy, who was standing there with us, said, "How about the head of each security team, the Board, and anyone else who wants to attend."

Rick said, "That's what I was thinking, please pass the word to meet in two hours."

Eddy has three main jobs, brewing beer and wine, growing pot, and pulling security duty. Ed used to be a full-time brewer of beer in the big city. Everyone likes Ed's beer so he is a popular guy. Ed likes pot more than anyone and once he starts smoking he becomes very weird. I don't know who is crazier, Eddy or Mark. Anyway, Mark and Ed have the pot under control and get along just fine. Ed won't tell anyone how he makes beer, keeping it a secret for some reason, maybe to make himself more popular or to feel needed. Ed is married and his wife does a lot of the farming in our community garden.

We have six security teams made up of 16 people each for a total of 96 people who can shoot. Each team has a team leader, meaning six people in the meeting plus the five Board of Directors which is made up of Rick as President, me as Vice President and Director of Security, Steve as Treasurer, Robbie as Member at Large and Bill as Secretary. The Security Team Leaders are Police Bob, Army Mike, Navy Ron, Marine Tommy, Deputy Matthews, and Big Steve, using the nicknames that everyone calls them. Rick would put up a notice at the town hall that anyone could attend the meeting but the final decisions would be made by the Board.

At the meeting, we decided to do a recon of the area to see just what this gang was up to and exactly where they were located in case we needed to attack them. The recon would be conducted by Tommy and me. If my son was going then I was going with him. Tonight would be perfect for this surveillance because there was no moon and the darkness would provide us excellent cover. Tommy was a Marine Scout Sniper and an expert at doing recon so I relied on him as we got ready, suited up, checked our weapons, gear, put on our camouflage paint, bulletproof vests and then duck-taped anything down that made noise.

We had about a mile to go to reach our destination with fairly good cover. The bad guys could be waiting along the way or lying in the brush watching us. Either way it would be dangerous. We drew a map and made a plan with set meeting points in case we became separated from each other.

Once we crossed the bridge and were beyond the car roadblock, we had to cross an open space of about 300 feet. The plan was that Tommy would take the west side of the road and I would take the east side of the road. That way if one of us was spotted we could set up a crossfire and cover each other. A line of trees and heavy mangroves on each side of the road would provide cover most of the way to the first buildings.

We crossed the bridge at 3 am, as the best time to sneak around is 2 to 4 am. That is when most people are in deep sleep. I was moving down the east side and Tommy down the west side of the road on the edge of the shrubs and mangrove trees. I could hardly see Tommy in the moonless night. He was about 100 feet across the road from me. We each had a radio to stay in touch. Clicking the transmit button three times meant stop and five times meant go. With this signal, the radio would hiss a static soft clicking noise. No talking unless it was necessary.

As we got within 400 yards of the first building I saw a person sitting on the edge of the road in a chair. I clicked three times to Tommy and he stopped. Using my night vision I saw this guy was asleep or had his eyes closed. I clicked five times to go. While Tommy proceeded I aimed my AR15 9mm at the guard's head. After Tommy was clear, he would cover me.

I had to pass within twenty feet of this guard. I held my breath and watched where I was walking so as not to make any noise, creeping along step-by-step until I was about one hundred feet past him. It was time for Tommy to cross the road over to my side, since the view was better on the east side of the street. Tommy slowly crawled on his belly across the road taking about 15 minutes, while I covered him. So far, so good, we had not been spotted.

I whispered to Tommy, "I think these guys are in one of the big four-story buildings and may have a shooter on the top floor. It's probably the one near the road."

This complex had about ten big buildings with two near the road, one on the east side and one on the west, so maybe they were in both buildings. As we sneaked around the buildings, keeping near the plants for cover, we spotted their cars at the one building on the east side of the road.

Tommy said quietly, "I want to go inside."

I replied, "Negative, too dangerous. Let's go back, we've got enough information."

Tommy nodded and we started back.

As we approached the guard sleeping in the road, he suddenly woke up when an owl screamed in the night. He stood up and I froze about 30 feet away from him. Tommy was on the other side of the road out of sight. I clicked three times on the radio. The guy looked around dazed and then he saw me on the edge of the mangroves and jumped to reach for his AK47. I popped him with my AR 9mm carbine three times, which of course made three loud bangs. He was no doubt dead, as I never miss with my AR15 9mm. It shoots like a BB gun with very little recoil.

We both started to run for the bridge, keeping close to the overgrowth. Tommy would run ahead about 50 feet since he was faster than me and then stop and look back, aiming his rifle to provide cover fire.

We were about halfway back and Tommy shouted, "Dad, keep running to the bridge, I will cover you. They're coming in a car."

I was so out of breath I couldn't speak or reply to him, but my brain was working overtime. I turned to see one car coming. That meant possibly three or four men.

I stopped, trying to regain my breath and replied, "Don't shoot, hide until they pass you. I am running in the middle of the road so they can see me."

"Ok, Dad," yelled Tommy.

I thought I could run faster on the road than in the dirt. I can make it. My hope was if they saw me in the road then they would drive right past Tommy, who was hidden in the mangroves, come after me and then we'd have them in a trap.

I knew Ron and Robbie would be there with more men and we would kill them if they came within range. I was huffing and puffing, running at full speed, slower than a turtle it seemed, with 40 pounds of gear on me.

I was tired and ready to fall. I stumbled as I got to the first cars in the roadblock. Robbie and Ron were there to meet me. I stumbled falling to my knees; Ron raced out and grabbed me, half-dragging me back up the bridge behind a car. I laid there and puked, trying to gain control of my breath. I thought, man, I have to quit smoking.

I run three miles four times a week but running with all that gear on, a bulletproof vest, 100 rounds of ammo, rifle, pistol, water and heavy boots was difficult. I am too old for this shit.

The car got closer and gunfire was flashing from the windows. Ron, Robbie and about ten others started shooting, firing everything they had, and the car came to a screeching halt about 200 feet from us. Gunfire stopped coming from the car. One dope jumped out of the car and started to run back down the road, trying to get away. I don't know how our bullets missed him as he ran out of effective range.

I got on the radio and called Tommy saying, "Bad guy coming toward you, take him out."

A few minutes later we heard one shot, which means one kill if Tommy fired it.

The radio hissed, "Got him, Dad. On my way back. Did you guys kill the rest of them?"

"I think so but check the car on your way back."

A few moments later, Tommy was jogging down the road and he stopped at the car, pulled out his Glock

9mm, and started shooting into it. He pulled the bodies out of the car and dragged them to the edge of the water. Hopefully the high tide would wash them out to sea.

Driving the car full of bullet holes over to us, Tommy said, "Some of those assholes were still alive but not now. I got us some more guns and ammo; here are three AK47 rifles and ten mags of ammo."

"Good job," I said, and I thanked God we made it back.

"What do we do now? They've still got us blocked in," Rick asked.

Tommy replied, "I have an idea; we have killed another five dope heads, cutting their numbers down to less than 30 men. I suggest we snipe them to kill more and after they lose another 10 or 15 guys, they may give up and leave. We don't need to go after them and breach the buildings. I can kill them at 700 yards away. That way we stay safe."

I replied, "I don't mind fighting in the open but going into their secured buildings is another matter."

We needed hand grenades and the Rangers gave us a boxful but breaching a building is risky and an easy way to get killed. I didn't want any of us to get hurt, let alone killed. The idea was to take out the bad guys and not end up dead in the process. We're not trained for breaching buildings. Tommy's idea was a good one and everyone agreed with it.

I asked Rick, "Can Tommy use your Cobb 50 to shoot right through the buildings?"

Rick said, "Yes, but I don't want to use all the ammo. I've only have 200 rounds."

A 50 caliber armor-piercing round will go through a car engine so blowing through a concrete wall is not a problem.

Tommy, the expert in this said, "Here is the plan; the shooting platform will be the back of my pickup truck. This way we can get the hell out of there quickly if needed. I will take the Cobb 50 and my sniper rifle for easy window shots. Just give me ten rounds of 50 cal. I would like two people for added protection armed with ARs; they can watch for men who may try to sneak up on us. I need another person for a spotter to scan windows and ground areas for targets to hit. If we do this once or twice a day we can kill ten more of those jerks. This will demoralize them and they will give up and leave. I want Robbie, Eddy and Amy for a spotter."

We all agreed and Tommy made ready his Toyota four-door, four-wheel drive Tundra pickup. Tommy thought it important to hit them right away as they might not be expecting it and would be looking for the four men we just killed. Robbie and Eddy would go with him for security and my daughter Amy would be his spotter.

Amy knows how to shoot and spot. She is an excellent shot and can handle any gun better than most men. Tommy and Amy are close and they think alike so she was the perfect choice but I didn't like putting her in danger. She is my little girl even if she is thirty-five years old.

I was wishing someone else had the balls to go, as I was just too tired. Another reason I didn't want her to go was that she was a nurse, an RN, and she was valuable to the whole group.

They started loading up the guns, ammo, gear and water, when all of a sudden, we heard a lot of rapid gunfire coming from the other end of the island called, "NO MAN'S LAND."

The radio crackled, "We are under attack, send help ASAP!" called Army Mike, who was on duty with three other men at the edge of NO MAN'S LAND.

THOMAS H. WARD

APRIL 19, 2025

It was dawn when Mike's radio call came in.

On the radio to Mike, I asked, "How many are you fighting?"

He replied, "About ten men and they came by boat and flanked us. We are between the four cars blocking the bridge. They are behind us in the toll booth and on the west side of the bridge. This is a serious situation and we could all be killed, you have to act fast."

Getting back on the radio, I told the other guards, "Watch for any boats; if they come within shooting range, shoot to kill. Mike, we are on the way. Everyone else be alert, at the ready, in case we need help."

Tommy, Eddy, Robbie and I were set to go. I asked Amy, "Please sit this one out."

She got out of the truck and we all jumped in. I could see Amy was disappointed not to get in the action, she is pretty much fearless.

As we were leaving Tommy told Rick, "Keep an eye on this bridge in case they try to attack here again."

Good point, this could be a two-pronged attack so we would be fighting on two fronts at once, which was not good.

Tommy shouted, "Everyone ready? Here we go!"

Tommy punched the gas and the 5.7 liter Tundra burned rubber for a few feet, as the truck sped forward.

Our island has two bridges, one on each end. The island is about one mile wide and two miles long. The main bridge in is an old-fashioned Bascule double-leaf drawbridge that can open and close by rising in the middle. This is the only way onto the island from the mainland, unless you come by boat.

The other bridge goes to No Man's Land, which use to be a county park with beaches. It is also an island and has no connection to the mainland. No one lives there except a few homeless people who have a trailer and want to be off the grid. There are five of them who help us tend the crops we grow there. In turn, we give them part of what we grow and also provide other foodstuffs. These people are harmless and have no weapons but will tell us if someone lands there by boat. We patrol NO MAN'S LAND everyday because we also hunt rabbits and fish there.

Speeding down the road, I told everyone in the truck, "Listen up. Mike and his three guys are trapped between the four cars on the bridge. The bad boys are at the toll booth and on the west side of the road. I suggest we stop and approach on foot from about 200 yards away so they don't see us."

Tommy replied, "Sounds good to me."

"Me too," agreed Robbie.

No comment came from Eddy. Eddy didn't like to fight and he needed more experience but he was willing to do his part.

I advised, "When we stop Ed, you stay behind and

act as the rear guard, staying near the truck but watch for bad guys and don't shoot us. I repeat, do not shoot in our direction. If you see anyone let me know right away, ok?"

Eddy, trying to sound military replied, "Roger that, boss."

Tommy drove off the road close to the undergrowth as we pulled up to within 200 yards.

We jumped out of the truck and I pointed to some bushes on the side of the road and instructed, "Ed this is a good place for you to stay. Robbie and I will stay on the west side and take out the toll booth. Tommy you secure the east side and provide a flanking move, also attacking the toll booth. After we clear it we will find more dopers on the west side of the road near the bridge."

Tommy answered, "Yes sir sounds like a good plan to me."

In the now strong daylight we walked toward the toll booth on the edge of the mangroves. Tommy was on the east side of the road in the shadow of the trees caused by the rising sun. We could clearly see the enemy shooting at Mike's team.

I radioed Mike, "We are here and are going to take the toll booth first and then go after the others."

Mike replied, "Hurry up! Big Dan is hit bad."

Tommy radioed, "Dad, I can see five guys and have a shot at all of them. Permission to fire?"

I responded, "If you got a clear shot, take it; kill them all if you can. Robbie and I will try to draw their fire."

From where Tommy was he could see three sides, east, north and south of the booth, while we could see the west and north side. So no matter what wall they hid behind we could shoot them. Robbie and I found a small drainage ditch to hunker down in for cover and waited for Tommy to shoot. We heard two rapid shots and two guys fell. We started to fire at the three remaining men and they fired back at us, bullets slamming into the ground all around us and zipping overhead.

At this point they didn't know Tommy was shooting at them. I heard another two shots from the 308 and Tommy called me, the radio hissing, "Dad, two more dead, that's four now. The last man is running for the water."

Bam! I heard his gun fire again. "I am coming over now, the last man got away!" Tommy shouted.

Mike overheard us when we talked on the radio. He keyed in, "Good shooting guys but I got bad news. Big Dan is dead and Sammy is wounded but not seriously. The remaining men are now under the bridge. I don't know if there are four or five of them. I think they are trying to take off in their boat."

We hurried to the bridge where Mike was shooting at the boat with four men in it trying to escape. He got one but the boat was fast and moved in a zigzag pattern to avoid being hit. Tommy rested his rifle on the bridge railing and fired three shots, making three more dead. The boat kept going for a while until at about 600 yards, when Tommy shot the motor and it ignited. We just let it burn and float away.

I radioed Eddy, "Bring up the truck fast, we got wounded here."

Eddy came zooming up and almost ran us over. Jumping out of the truck, he ran over to see who was hurt and started to sob when he saw Big Dan dead. He asked, "What happened?"

Only Mike knew what happened and he did not reply. Sammy was in pain and shock and didn't speak one word. He was going to pass out from the loss of blood. Eddy tied a rope around his arm right above the wound to stop the blood flow.

We loaded Sammy and Big Dan's body into the back of the truck. It was a sad day, the first time anyone in our compound had been killed.

I asked Mike, "What the hell happened? How did those guys sneak up on you?"

Mike answered, "I have no excuse. We were playing cards and were tired. Dan had a bottle of whiskey and we all had a few drinks. We were listening to music. You know how boring it is doing guard duty."

I gave him a disgusted look and radioed to our HQ, "We are on the way back. Sammy is wounded with a bullet through the arm and Dan is dead. Have Doc and Amy ready to treat Sammy."

A long time ago Big Dan was married but his wife died in a car accident. They had no kids so Dan had no one to call family but us, his friends. He moved here from Ohio where he sold cars. We would honor him for his sacrifice.

Mike wanted to resign as a team leader and leave security altogether.

He told me, "I need to step down. I feel so bad about Dan."

I said, "Mike, listen to me, you are a good man;

you made a mistake but it was not all your fault. I believe that when your time's up, it's up. We need your skill and leadership, it's imperative to our security. You are a key man and I think you will be more careful in the future. This is life and death here, just like being in a war. Hell, you could get killed from a snake bite. I don't need to preach to you, a 20-year Army vet. I just ask that you handle Big Dan's funeral and bury him at sea. First, get back to work by picking two replacement men then get back to the bridge asap because as we have no guards there now. Also dump the scumbags' bodies into shark channel."

The shark channel is what we call the water that flows between the two islands because if you try to swim across it most likely Bull sharks will attack you. Bull sharks are the most aggressive sharks around, they're even worse than Mako and Great Whites. I know of at least three people that have died swimming in that water.

Speaking of snakes, we had rattlesnakes and rats everywhere. Sometimes if we saw a snake we'd kill it, skin it, gut it and eat it. You have to be careful when cutting off the head not to let the fangs touch you or it could mean death. You need to take the head and throw it in the deep water or bury it so no one else comes in contact with this demon. It tastes like chicken. Yummy! Snakes are good to have around as they eat the rats and mice, so we don't kill many.

A while back I killed two snakes that somehow got onto my patio. We have little Pigmy rattlesnakes, which have no rattle and are about 12 inches long but resemble a big rattlesnake. When I first saw the snakes they looked like sticks lying there and were not moving.

I looked closer and they coiled up and struck at me. Only poisonous snakes do that. So I took my flat-bladed shovel, cut off their heads and threw them in the water. I worry about my wife and little dogs. The dogs do go after snakes when they see them but not close enough to get bit.

Big Dan had a short funeral with a 21-gun salute the same day. We need to get rid of bodies fast here, with the oppressive heat, as we don't have freezers big enough to store bodies. Mike started out the funeral talking about Dan; they had been friends for 20 years, like most of us living here. Then others stood and told their own, sometimes funny stories of times they had spent with Dan. Dan was covered with an American flag as he was a true American patriot. Everyone was there except for the sixteen people who were on guard duty. Most of us cried as we put his body on the boat to be buried at sea, as was his wish. Robbie and Eddy took him out to sea about a mile, weighted down the body with concrete blocks,   and slid him overboard with a prayer.

Everyone is buried at sea here because we have no room for a cemetery and don't want dead bodies buried near us. The coyotes will dig them up and eat them. Coyotes pose a danger. They came here in the year 2000. They are fast, smart and eat anything, even people, but they usually try to make easy kills of rabbits, cats and dogs. We try to shoot them on sight but they are elusive and roam mainly at night. One ran down the middle of the street in broad daylight the other day and it went by so fast most people didn't see it.

Tommy, Robbie, and I went back to the main bridge after the funeral. It was about 2 pm and so hot you could cook an egg on the blacktop road. You always sweat here; there is little relief from the heat and sun. Your clothes stick to you and are drenched in sweat. You find some shade and try to stay cool. The slightest breeze is a welcome relief.

To my surprise Rick was not there but Bill was, with nine security people. Bill is the Association's Secretary and not much of a fighter because he is too clumsy. He used to be a computer programmer. He even has trouble loading a gun, but he can shoot one fairly well. He has a good eye.

I asked Bill, "Where is Rick?"

"Rick went home. He did not feel well and ask me to take over. Nothing has happened here, all is quiet," Bill replied.

I said, "Thank God. Have you seen any gang members?"

Bill answered, "Yes, a few came down the road in a car but did not challenge us; they stopped about 300 yards down the road and then drove away. Maybe they decided to leave this area altogether."

"I have only slept one hour in the past two days. I am tired, hungry, and need a garden hose shower. If anything happens, radio me," I told Bill.

"Tommy and Robbie, you coming with me?"

Tommy said, "Yeah, Dad, we need to discuss our next action plan."

I replied, "After I eat, shower and have one of

Eddie's beers."

Robbie said, "How about we come over around 6 pm? I'll go tell the rest of the Board to meet at 6:30 pm in the bar."

"Ok with me," Tommy said.

I replied, "Ditto."

I went back to my home and my wife, Hemmi, cooked up some fried fish and made a salad with fruit, and green beans, all grown right here. I ate four fish fillets and drank four beers. Even warm beer tastes good. You get use to it.

Hemmi is an excellent cook and also a great shot. She shoots her Ruger 22 caliber flat slab stainless steel, six-inch barrel target pistol, with a red dot scope. She can hit a golf ball almost every time at 50 yards.

Hemmi asked, "Everything ok now? I was worried about you not eating and being gone so long. What I am going to do if you get killed like Dan?"

"Honey don't worry, I am not going to get killed if I can help it," I replied, in an effort to put her at ease.

I gave her a little kiss on the cheek and asked, "What did you do today?"

"Nothing new, just picked lettuce, fruit, and cleaned fish for dinner. Oh, I helped Doc Scott and Amy fix up Sammy at the clinic. That was intense but he will be fine. It was a clean hole through his arm. He may lose some movement, however."

I commented, "Well, at least he is alive and he will be relieved from security duty for a few weeks, but his wife won't be happy having him around the house all day."

We both laughed at that comment.

I never let Hemmi take security guard duty as she has no experience in gun battles; she does not have the proper training. But if she had to, Hemmi would kill to protect our family.

Most of the time Hemmi hangs around with Amy; they either work at the medical clinic, garden, or are busy cooking a meal for the family. They tend to the more or less everyday life necessities, as well as spend time teaching the small number of kids we have here, the youngest being ten years old. We have three teachers who instruct the kids on freedom, the Bill of Rights and the Constitution. In addition, we teach them reading, writing, math, history, fishing, hunting and farming. An old-fashioned education never hurt anyone.

We do have some good points besides the sun and clean air; for one thing, food is fairly easy to obtain. We have orange, lemon, grapefruit, avocado, and coconut trees, which yield a lot of fruit for about six months out of the year. We have many gardens and grow all varieties of vegetables, enough to feed everyone here and more. Great fishing is right off shore, or further out in a boat if you want bigger fish. You name it, we fish it. We have 20 fulltime fishermen, as we need about a pound of fish per person a day. For 500 people this is 500 pounds, meaning each man needs to bring in 25 pounds a day. Actually, it is not so hard to catch 25 pounds of fish as one grouper is usually up to 30 pounds. King fish and snapper can run 15 pounds. We smoke fish and grill it over an open fire. We have rabbits, squirrels, and birds to eat. The only bird I like is dove and we have a lot of them, for some reason. They taste like chicken.

Speaking of chicken, one day a chicken farmer arrived in a truck loaded with chickens and the necessary equipment to build a hen house. He also had a couple of roosters for breeding. He asked if he could join our group and in turn he would supply us eggs and chickens. This chicken farmer loves his chickens. The chicken farm is located in NO MAN'S LAND as the birds make a lot of noise and need room. Chickens can be dangerous. Close contact with them brought about the bird flu years ago in China. People living and eating with a bunch of chicken excrement nearby is not healthy. Now we eat eggs almost every day and sometimes a fried chicken. We draw numbers to see who the lucky ones are that get the chicken. The coyotes are always after the chickens so the pen is guarded.

I told Hemmi, "I've got a 6:30 meeting."

Just then Robbie and Tommy walked in and asked, "You ready to go?"

I put my Glock in my hostler, grabbed my AR 15, and kissed Hemmi goodbye saying, "See you later, I will be home tonight."

My decision was to leave the gang alone for now. The gang just lost another eight men, bringing their force down to 20 or 22 people. They had no food and sooner or later they would have to give up and leave for greener pastures. I explained this to Tommy and Robbie and they agreed with me. The plan would be do nothing for now. We just lost one man and one was wounded, we needed to rest.

Tommy replied, "Today we can recuperate but tomorrow I want to do another recon to verify if they are still there."

I thought, *Oh no!* I remained quiet as did Robbie while we drove to the meeting.

Everyone was at the meeting except Rick.

I asked, "Anyone seen Rick?"

Doc Scott answered, "Rick is sick, he was a fever, I think he has malaria so you are in charge for now."

"I had malaria, or may still have it. Give him some quinine water and that will put the bug into remission," I told the Doc.

"Really, that will cure him?"

"No, it will not cure him but he will feel better right away and it may save his life. Make sure he drinks a quart of it."

The Doc left the meeting to search for tonic water. Doc Scott is a trauma surgeon and good at fixing bullet wounds and broken body parts, but not good at diagnosing a disease.

Bugs are everywhere and at night we are eaten up by the mosquitoes. There are 3,500 different species of mosquitoes. They can carry all kinds of nasty bugs that will kill us if not treated. Years ago I did contract malaria when I went to Southern China. The mosquitoes bit me and about a week later I started feeling like I had a fever. My muscles and joints ached. I went to the Mayo Clinic and they confirmed that I had a low level case of malaria, a less dangerous strain. To combat malaria you need to drink quinine, also called tonic water. For some reason this puts the disease into remission. When it comes back you drink some gin and tonic. You need to drink about a quart of tonic water to get it back into remission. The British discovered the use of quinine in the late 1890s; hence, when stationed in an area with a malaria problem they would drink a gin and tonic every day.

In the old days the county would spray to kill the little bloodsuckers, but not anymore. They can drive a man nuts buzzing around looking for a tender place to suck blood. You need to wear long-sleeve shirts, pants, and a hat with netting to protect your face. Everyone gets bit. Standing water puddles are their breeding sites. To keep them at bay at night we start wood fires and the smoke helps. Problem is the smoke gives me a bad headache. I go to my screened-in porch and sleep there free from bugs and snakes. It is cooler than sleeping in the house.

"I call this meeting to order," I said. "We will discuss what actions we should take against the so-called gang. Does anyone have a suggestion or idea?"

Bob asked me, "Whatever happened to the Rangers?"

"I don't know, maybe they were delayed. We can't count on the Rangers for help, so it's up to us."

Tommy jumped in saying, "I propose we do nothing tonight, just keep our guard up and everyone stay at the ready. Tomorrow night I will do another recon but I need a volunteer to go with me. My Dad has done enough. I need someone young, fresh and ready to go."

Anyone can attend the meeting and speak up at anytime. From near the door a voice called out, "I will go with you, Tommy."

It was Carlos. He came here from Puerto Rico

years ago and was in the Army for four years.

Tommy said, "Great, then it is Carlos and me."

My son-in-law, Jim added, "I'll go too, you may need extra eyes."

"Great," Tommy said. "Jim, Carlos, and I will make up the team."

I stated, "With no further business, the meeting is adjourned. Beers for everyone."

Jim is a great shot. He pulls guard duty but his main job is making repairs to equipment, cars, boats— you name it, Jim can fix it. Everyone relies on him as our Mr. Fix-it. I am lucky to have such a great son-in-law. I call him Jim Bo.

I know Carlos and he is a good, brave man. He is Catholic, loves God, and prays continuously. He and his wife Sandy are freedom lovers and hate when the government tells you what to do. I was ok with Carlos going with Tommy, but I also had another idea which may be better.

I will tell them about my new idea later as I need to rest now.

APRIL 20, 2025

The sun is up and it is another hot day. Hemmi cooked me eggs with smoked fish and cut up some oranges. Simple, but good, healthy food. I put on my bulletproof vest, my Kydex hostler, and Glock. I grabbed my AR 15 9mm carbine and an AR 15 H bar rifle chambered for 5.56 NATO rounds with a 4X lowlight scope. It is good for 500 yards.

My wife asked, "What are you doing today?"

I told her, "We have another recon tonight. Tommy, Jim, and Carlos…maybe I will go along. But I've got to go to the bridge now, see you later."

She commented as I walked out the door, "Be safe you big dope!"

"A man's got to do what a man's got to do. Bye, I love ya," I said softly as the back door closed behind me.

As I approached the bridge everyone was looking down the road, with ten men on guard duty. Jeff was in charge overnight. The guard had just changed at 7 am, but some of the guys still hung around and were also looking down the road.

I asked Jeff, the team leader, "What's going on?"

Then I looked down the road and saw a car about 100 yards away. That's what everyone was watching. I asked out loud to anyone, "How long has that been there?"

Plumber Greg said, "It came sometime in the night, no one saw it approach."

I said, "Is everyone blind, sleeping or what? How can you let a car sneak up and get that close?" This car would throw a whammy at the recon for tonight unless we learned more about it.

No need to tell you what Greg the Plumber does. He is a good person and helps anyone with plumbing problems, from fixing broken water lines to unclogging drains. He has no military experience and sometimes makes quick decisions and judgments that could put him and others in danger. Greg is a hard worker and you can trust him to get any job done, plus he keeps his word.

I advised Greg and the others, "Maybe this is a trap, a booby trap. The car could blow up when we get near it. They might have explosives rigged in it and could set them off by a radio or cell phone or just by opening the door."

Greg replied, "Duh, you think so?"

No one here knows much about explosives. This was a dangerous situation. I looked at the car through my rifle scope trying to discern wires or telltale signs of a bomb. It appeared to be just an empty car. I thought, *This seems to be a Trojan horse, we need to be careful.*

I radioed Tommy, "Wake up and bring the Cobb 50 to the bridge right away, we have a situation."

"Yes, Sir, be right there," Tommy replied.

Twenty minutes later Tommy arrived with the Cobb and saw the problem. The car's motor was pointed directly at us. I said, "Tommy that could be a car bomb. What do we do about it?"

Tommy said, "I can shoot that car from here and start it on fire. If there are any explosives in it the fire will cause them to go off."

I said, "Great, start shooting."

If we didn't get rid of this car it would render our recon by land impossible and we might have to conduct it by boat, which is risky because any time you are on the water you are an easy target.

Tommy chambered a round into the Cobb.

The Cobb 50 BMG is a 50-caliber rifle, shooting a Browning machine gun round that can go through steel, even an engine block. It can enter through one side of a car, come out the other side, and kill someone. The BMG has a muzzle velocity of 1,900 miles per hour or 2,800 feet per second. The BMG bullet is ½ inch in diameter and nearly four inches long. I call it the Superman Bullet. The Cobb is a semi automatic rifle, built just like an AR 15 but bigger and has a ten round magazine.

Tommy put the Cobb on some sand bags for support and took aim at the car's engine, squeezing the trigger, sending the superman bullet … Kaboom! The whole front of the car exploded in a massive fire ball, sending pieces of metal at us and a shock wave of wind, as we all ducked. If we would have been any closer one of us could have been killed. The sound was so loud it almost blew out my eardrums. Now we had a burning wreck sitting in the middle of the road with black smoke billowing high into the sky but at least it was no longer a bomb threat. We'd just let the fire burn itself out which would probably take most of the day.

Tommy looked down the road through the Cobb rifle scope and yelled, "They're coming! Everyone get ready."

We all looked down the road and I saw six cars. Without warning, Tommy fired the Cobb again…BAM! BAM! BAM! Three shots in a row and three cars exploded. The other three cars stopped and quickly backed up to get out of rifle range.

People were jumping out of the blazing cars and running for cover. Tommy shot three of them with the Cobb and I guess about nine of them got away. It doesn't matter where you are hit with a Superman bullet, it kills you. Hitting you in the leg or shoulder it blows those body parts right off into big chunks of meat and you go into shock, bleed out, and die.

I think the assholes heard the explosion and thought we were all dead and this was their chance to breach our roadblock. They had no clue that we were waiting for them and ready to take out more of these creeps. They had no idea we had a Cobb 50, which can stop a car in its tracks. These guys were really pissing me off. They didn't even know they had already lost the war; probably because they were all doped up and had no idea what they were doing, no logic, no reasoning, the dumb bastards.

Since they were out the range of the AR and 308 rifles, no one else got off a shot. We all just started to laugh and Deputy Matthews shouted out, "Great shooting, Tommy!"

Tommy had just dropped another three guys, bringing the total number of junkies over there down to less than twenty and he blew up three of their cars.

I commented to everyone, "The question is what do we do now? Is the recon patrol still on? Should we wait? I am out of ideas and think we need to regroup before acting. We need to push that burning car off the road all the way into the water if possible. The three cars down the road we'll just leave at that location and hope the coyotes eat the dead bodies."

Rick heard the explosion and drove down to the bridge. We told him what happened and that we used four rounds of BMG in the process of dropping these guys.

Rick said, "Great shooting Tommy, you can have the Cobb 50 and all my ammo. You are a better shooter than I'll ever be."

"Thanks," Tommy replied.

I asked Rick, "How do you feel?"

"I am ok now. Thanks for telling the Doc what to give me because he had no idea how to treat this. I appreciate it buddy but what are we going to do now?"

"I suggest we do nothing as there is no urgent need for us to leave the island, so we wait them out. Let's get some lunch and think about it."

We jumped in Tommy's truck and drove to the bar.

I felt like something was missing, my shadow. I asked Tony the barkeeper, "Have you seen Mark around?"

Tony replied, "No, not today."

I got on the radio announcing, "All security stations: If anyone has seen Mark, give me a call. I've got a job for him."

Chris, one of the security guards, clicked his radio and said, "Yeah, a job dumping bodies into the water. Ha, ha."

I gave no reply and Rick laughed.

Mark would disappear for one or two days at a time. He wouldn't tell anyone where he was going or what he was doing. Mark was like a shadow. He would come and go without anyone seeing him. No one paid attention to him. I was a little concerned because Mark didn't think like a normal person and if he got some idea in his head he might act on it, even if it put him in danger.

Rick and I were enjoying a meal of smoked fish and drinking tonic water when Tommy walked in and said, "I suggest we go back to my original plan of sniping them from the back of my truck. I suggest we hit them now. It's 2 pm and hot as usual, so the scumbags will most likely be inside, out of the sun."

Rick replied, "Ok, after we eat and down a few cool drinks."

We decided to go snipe after 4 pm. That way the sun's angle would be to our advantage, if we stayed on the west side of the road, near the mangrove trees.

We were slowly driving down the dirt strip near the bushes, when Tommy announced, "Is that Mark's bike?"

I saw it too and responded, "Yes, maybe Mark is nearby. Get out and look."

I drove while Tommy and Robbie paced the roadway, searching through the thick vegetation. Tommy yelled, "Dad, here he is! I think he is dead!"

I jumped out of the truck, my heart pounding, and ran about ten feet to reach Tommy's location. Looking down I saw Mark lying in the bushes all cut up in a puddle of blood. His hands and feet were duct-taped and he had a piece of duct tape across his mouth. He was a bloody mess and had a note pinned to his chest by a knife. I recognized the knife, it was Mark's fishing knife.

The note read, "Feed your buddy to the fish." I pulled the tape off his face and cut the tape off his hands and feet. They roughed him up real good, even skinning half his face off; I could see his jaw bone. He was a mess of blood and dirt with black and blue marks, and his face was swollen beyond recognition. I could hardly tell it was my poor buddy.

I was looking at his beaten face and said, "Hey buddy can you hear me? Who did this?"

Mark couldn't open his eyes as they were swollen shut. I gripped his hand and assured him, "Mark you're going to be fine, we'll get you back to the Doc and Amy to patch you up."

Mark moaned in a whisper, "Jack… they got me buddy … they killed me dead. Get 'em for me."

I squeezed his hand as he was coughing up blood. Then Mark whispered, "Fish food."

He gasped and took a deep breath and went limp. They cut him all over and he had bled profusely. They left him for dead knowing we would find him. I wasn't sure if Mark would make it with the extensive body wounds and beating he took. They probably tried to get information out of him but I knew Mark would never talk. We lifted Mark into the back of the truck and drove to the clinic as fast as we could.

I got on the radio to Amy and instructed her, "Amy, get the Doc, we are bringing Mark to the clinic. He's been beaten and stabbed."

Stab wounds are the worst as you don't know how much damage has been done internally and we had no X-ray machines or any type of scanners. I know what damage a sharp knife can do. I always carry one with me. Years ago when I lived in Ohio, a junkie broke into our house when we were sleeping. My wife and two kids were sound asleep in the house. I am a very light sleeper and the slightest noise can wake me up. I had heard something. I sat up in bed and listened carefully. I heard the stairs creaking. I knew the sounds of this house like the back of my hand since I grew up in it. I knew every creak a stair would make as my brother and I used to play hide and seek in this big old Victorian.

I put my hand over my wife's mouth and woke her up, holding my index finger to my mouth, signaling her to remain silent. I whispered, "There is someone in the house, call the police and be quiet." Back in those days we didn't have 911 so you called the operator by dialing zero and asked to be connected to the police. I didn't have a gun because my wife did not let me keep one in the house, claiming it was safer for the kids.

Moving with stealth to my dresser, I pulled out the bowie knife that my dad purchased for me when I was 12 years old to use when we went camping. I kept this knife very sharp and it was the only item that I had of my father's. I recall us going to the hunting store and he let me pick out any knife I wanted; it was a big deal because Dad never bought us anything. My heart was beating a mile a minute, as I listened again. The creaking was coming closer to the top of the stairs. I slipped on my pants and quietly closed the three bedroom doors. I was now standing at the top of the stairs, out of sight around a corner. I would be able to see his foot when he reached the top of the stairs. That was when I would strike and try to run my knife through his heart or die trying. I was praying he didn't have a gun. My dad always told me: Don't bring a knife to a gun fight.

I could hardly breathe and my heart was racing so fast I could hear it. I heard his steps coming up so very slowly, and then I saw his foot touch the top of the stairs. I leaped at him and screamed, plunging my knife into his chest as hard as I could. We both fell back down the stairs and I landed on top of him. My knife was stuck in his chest, all right, but not in the heart, it was in his shoulder near the collar bone, above the heart. I feared he had a gun but did not see one. Looking around I only saw a small pocket knife. He moaned, my wife came out of the bedroom and screamed. I told her to shut the hell up and go open the door for the cops, whom I assumed were on the way. She stepped over us crying while racing down the stairs. I admit; I was upset at my wife for not allowing me to have a gun in the house and it almost got us all killed. I was scared and shaking.

I sat on top of this junkie holding him down with my knife still in his shoulder. He started to moan; suddenly he opened his eyes and tried to push me off. He was doped up and strong. I punched him in the face as hard as I could several times hurting my hand, while grinding my knife blade around in his shoulder, as his blood pumped out. Finally, he stopped moving.

The cops took my knife for evidence but I never got it back.

At the Med Clinic Amy saw Mark and just started to weep. Doc Scott said he never seen anything this bad before. We put him on the table and Doc checked his heart.

Doc stated with sorrow in his voice, "I'm sorry, Mark has passed. There is no heart beat, no signs of life."

The room was silent except for Amy's sobbing and we hugged each other. Crazy Mark, my shadow, my go-to guy, dead at the hand of those dirt balls. I was the last one to leave the room and I promised Mark I would get the bastards that did this to him. They would indeed be fish food.

I pulled Mark's knife out of his chest, wiped off the blade and put it in my pocket, saying out loud, "I will never forget you buddy."

I couldn't help but wonder how Mark got out of the compound and across the bridge without anyone seeing him leave.

Robbie arranged the funeral and it was held just like the one for Big Dan. Everyone attended and this time I spoke about Mark's life and so did Robbie. I said the Lord's Prayer for him. Robbie and I, along with Tommy, took him out to sea for his burial.

As we lowered his body into the ocean Tommy said, "We've got to put an end to these guys."

Robbie commented in anger, "If I get one alive I

am going to do a lot worse to them than they did to Mark."

I replied, "Robbie, we aren't animals like them. We'll just kill'em and feed them to the fish. God will give them their just punishment."

We arrived back at the dock just as the sun set and headed to the bar to have a drink for Mark.

Tomorrow we will go hunting.

THOMAS H. WARD

APRIL 21, 2025

Rick called a meeting in the morning to review our plans. It was a heated debate as we do have rules of engagement that should be followed.

Rules of Engagement: 1. Only shoot someone who has a gun or weapon and is an immediate threat. 2. Never shoot blindly at a target ... meaning you must be able to see your target so as not to endanger innocent people. 3. Never take unnecessary risks. 4. Always be sure who you are shooting.

Deputy Matthews said, "I can't let you guys blow holes through a wall not knowing who is inside the building. So you can't shoot anyone without a clear shot and must verify they have a gun in their hand. What if there are innocent people with them?"

Most of the group agreed with Matthews and so did Tommy and I.

Robbie said, "That's bull shit; we know these guys cut Mark up and murdered him and Dan. If other people are in the building with them then whatever happens, too bad for them."

Matthews replied, "What if those people have no choice because they were kidnapped? It's true we don't know if they have any more slaves with them and thanks to Jack we saved five of them. So those are the rules of engagement we set up and they must be followed."

The punishment for not following the rules of engagement is removal from the security team and possible banishment from the compound for life. We do not have jails or a court system and since we are in a war-like state that is the best we can do. Anyone who fights another compound member runs the risk of being banned. The outside world is mean and scary so no one wants to risk that punishment. The jury we use is made up of the Board and the Security Team leaders, a 12-member jury of our peers. Disputes are also settled using our jury system. All-in-all everyone gets along fine most of the time. We maintain respect for each other.

So it was settled. We would not snipe at anyone we could not see, blow holes in the building or shoot anyone who didn't have a weapon. This was going to make our job a lot harder.

The plan was the same as before only this time we took Amy with us. Amy would help shoot using the 308, with Tommy on the big Cobb. Robbie and I would be security. Using a laser range finder we drove down the west side of the road in the dirt to within 600 hundred yards. That way both guns could be put in action. I turned the Tundra around with the bed facing the one building where we believed most of them were staying.

Robbie and I fanned out and watched the road and large shrubs and trees for possible movement.

It wasn't long before I heard the 308 Amy was

using fire a round. On the radio she said, "I got one through the window; he had a gun and was looking at us though a scope."

No one said a word. Then we heard shots come from the building and we ducked but the bullets were about 200 yards short and landed in the ground with soft thuds. I guess Amy's shot got their attention. We clearly had them out-gunned.

About two hours passed. No one else popped their heads up for us to target. I looked down the road and could see what appeared to be a little girl walking towards us. I looked through my rifle scope and she seemed to be about ten years old. She wore a backpack, the kind kids carry their lunch and books in when going to school. As she got closer she began to run towards us but the gang started shooting at her and bullets were dancing all around her. Amy and Tommy began shooting back at heads in the windows. The little girl was about 200 yards away when Amy sprang up and started to rush towards her.

I screamed, "Amy, no! Wait she might have a bomb planted on her!"

Amy kept running towards her and I jumped up and ran for Amy; Robbie was right behind me.

I shouted, "Amy, take her into the water to cover the backpack! Putting it underwater is the only way to block a radio or cell phone signal if she has a bomb."

Amy is a fast runner and she scooped up the little girl and jumped into the bay, submerging the backpack while we were all providing cover fire.

Amy called out to me, "Dad, she has a bomb tied to her, I need a knife!"

I ran as fast as I could to Amy; I always carry my Black Bear Cold Steel Bowie fighting knife. As I jumped into the water I only had a few steps to get to them. The little girl was crying. While keeping the pack submerged, I cut through the ropes like butter with my Black Bear. I swam with the pack, holding it underwater, for about 50 feet and tried to bury it in the mucky bottom but it wouldn't sink. Then while trying to dig a hole in the bottom my foot hit an old metal crab trap stuck in the muck. I tied the pack to it hoping it would not surface and swam like hell to shore. Metal crab traps are big and heavy, it was just what I needed.

In the salt water there are creatures that can hurt you, like sting rays and jelly fish. If stung by jelly fish you need to pour urine on the site to stop the stinging. I know this works well since I have used the urine treatment myself. Sting rays have an arrow or barb at the end of their tail and they swing the tail and stick you with the arrow. It hurts like hell but is not a serious injury. We also have sharks in the shallow and deep water. Years ago a man jumped in the water right off his dock and landed on top of an eight-foot bull shark, which promptly bit him in half, killing him on the spot. I stay away from the water as much as possible.

I waded out and sprinted to the truck along with the others, jumping in the vehicle, and we all headed back to the bridge. Amy was cradling the little girl in her arms. Amy was never able to have kids but she loves them.

She was telling her, "You're ok now, don't worry. Don't cry; you are safe with us."

The little girl was sobbing, "I want my mommy."

When we arrived back at the bridge we took her to the med clinic. She was a skinny little thing, clearly suffering from hunger and Amy gave her fish, beans, and fruit, which she gobbled up in a hurry.

Amy asked her, "Where is your mommy?"

She replied, "My mommy is back there," pointing toward the building she came from.

"What is your name?"

"Shanda Jones," she replied.

Shanda was safe now and able to fill her little tummy. She was tired and starting to fall asleep. I watched her little eyes close as Amy wrapped her in her arms and took her home to a safe place to sleep for the night. We could ask her more questions tomorrow but now she needed to rest.

A few of us sat around the main campfire downtown talking about how these people were willing to blow up a little girl to gain entrance into our compound. What dirt bags they were. What lowlifes they were to use a little girl by putting a bomb on her back? It was clear we were dealing with some dangerous and evil people that would resort to any measure to get what they want. Were they really that crazy? Maybe little Shanda could shed some light on this tomorrow after a good night's sleep.

I was thinking to myself, *I want them all dead.*

THOMAS H. WARD

April 22, 2025

The next day Amy came to our house with Shanda. Hemmi gave the child a lot of attention and the little girl ate a lot. The cutie seemed happy being with us. No one asked her any questions and she could relax here, not fearing for her life. Amy and Hemmi took her on a tour of our compound and she drank her first Coke and had her first taste of chocolate, which was not common even for us but someone had been saving the candy and decided to give it to her.

We didn't go sniping and stood down for the time being. Shanda was our main concern and everyone wanted to meet her and show her love. She brought an infusion of new life, new hope, a reminder of what it is to be innocent. It made us all start to think about others that were out there in need of food and shelter.

How many other kids were living in that cruel world with no hope? It broke my heart to think about it. It made us all wonder what we were doing to improve the situation for mankind. What were we doing to the little kids who had no concept of why people were fighting and killing each other? How could we make a difference?

I remained in the background as Amy and Hemmi played with her.

Later that day Amy asked her, "What is your

mommy's name?"

"Her name is the same as mine," Shanda said.

"Why did you come out yesterday and walk down the road to us?" Amy asked.

"Because Mommy told me to go over the bridge and get some food. Everyone wants to have food. I could take some back to Mommy. She is hungry too."

"Shanda, where is your daddy and what is his name?" Amy inquired, in a soft voice.

"My daddy is Big Jim. I don't know where Daddy is," replied Shanda, while smiling at Amy.

The three of us just looked at each other in disbelief. Stunned, I got up and left the room. I killed her daddy.

APRIL 23, 2025

I woke up and thought *Big Jim, the guy I killed, was her father!* Now she had no father and didn't know what would happen to her mother.

I started to wonder was the bomb a fake? Did her Mother allow to her come to us so she could be saved? That way the other gang members would not be suspicious. I was pretty sure the mother did send her out but not to blow us up it was to save Shanda's life.

Maybe she just wanted her daughter to have something to eat and a safe place to stay, now that she had no one like Big Jim to protect her. Maybe she thought it was better to be with us than the gang. This theory could be correct, and if it was, maybe her mother was not a dirt bag like her father. The only way to find out was to verify if that bomb was real or not.

It was about 10:30 am when all of a sudden I heard choppers coming. I rushed outside and saw the UH-60 Black Hawks fly directly overhead about 200 feet in the air. They were too many to count but I guessed there were about twenty of them. Two Black Hawks circled back and landed downtown near the Fire Station, which always flies the American Flag. The rest flew to the south toward NO MAN'S LAND. The Rangers were back, thank God!

I jumped into my truck with Tommy, Robbie, and Eddy. We raced to meet the Rangers just a few minutes down the street. Arriving, I saw Rick was already there along with Captain Sessions, a full-bird Colonel and a one-star General, along with a four-man security detail dressed in black. These were the General's security guards and they are real pros at what they do. There were also four other Rangers who I assumed were assigned to the Colonel under Captain Sessions.

We got out of the truck and walked up next to Rick. We all stood there in a straight line; Rick, Tommy, Eddy, Robbie, Mathews, and I.

Captain Sessions approached in the lead and said, "Hello gentlemen, it is good to see you once again. I would like to introduce my commanding officers, General Harper and Colonel Turner."

They went down the line shaking hands and we each introduced ourselves and told them our positions.

When the General stepped up to Tommy he said, "Are you Tommy Gunn, the Marine Sniper with 45 confirmed kills?"

Tommy replied, "Yes sir General, retired Marine now sir."

General Harper said, "It is an honor to meet a Silver Star winner."

The men in black were watching everything and everyone, forming a protective circle around the group. Three of them carried M4 carbines and one carried a SAW M249, which is a Squad Automatic Weapon, a light machine gun that holds a 100-round drum of 5.56 bullets.

Rick suggested, "Let's go into the church and talk in the shade, out of the bright sun and heat."

Sessions agreed, "Good idea."

One of the security men said, "Sir, we have to check the church first."

Two men went inside for five minutes and then called out, "General Harper Sir, it's all clear."

They followed us inside the church to the small conference room.

General Harper got down to business saying, "Gentlemen, let's not beat around the bush our country is in a serious state. Captain Sessions told me about your compound, how you run things and follow the Constitution of the United States. As you may know the President has declared a state of emergency invoking the Executive Order 13603, which basically declares the government owns all property, homes, guns, money, and even your kids.

"Gentlemen, we Rangers do not believe that order to be lawful or Constitutional and therefore will not follow it. We have put out a warrant for the arrest of the President for treason. When I say we I mean all Special Forces, Rangers, Delta Force, Green Berets, Seals, Marines and Air Force special ops. The rest of the Military is standing down for now. As you may know the President has the Federal Police Force under the Secret Service, a force of about 50,000 men, protecting him and the Congress in Washington. Make no mistake, we will arrest or eliminate anyone who may stand in our way. We have to regain control of our country.

"We intend to replace all members of Congress who are communists, and hold new elections sometime in the future. In addition the heads of the FBI, CIA, NSA, IRS, EPA, etc., and the entire Cabinet will be charged with treason for following his orders."

The President started a draft but not for the military, it is for the new Federal Police Force or FPF. Their job would be to start green safe zones in the cities and guard the electric power plants and water supplies. They were to keep things running and generally enforce the laws. The Federal Police have all the same weapons, trucks, and tanks that the Army does. There were now 50,000 new police officers. Even this number could not control the situation. The President put into effect Presidential Executive Order 13603, which to everyone's surprise, declares that all property belongs to the Federal government. They could tell you where to live and where to work.

"We operate under SOCOM based in Tampa, commanded by four-star General McNab. Our job is to secure a base of operations to gain control of the west coast of Florida. We want to put a base here and I assume you all would agree to this in short order as my Rangers are on the way. I just had 80 men land at what you call No Man's Land. We plan to have 580 Rangers based here within the next five days, most are coming by truck with supplies and so forth. The Rangers are from the 3rd Battalion of the 75th Ranger Regiment and also the 7th Special Forces group. Both are under SOCOM, Special Operations Command.

"I would like to house some families here for protection as they are in great danger of being arrested by the Federal Police Force. There are about 250 wives and children. Now, any questions or comments?"

I asked, "How will you remove the President?"

"Our forces will move on Washington and arrest the President, his communist cabinet or anyone else we have identified as a communist in the Executive Branch. This will include any affiliated Senator or Congressman. They will all be put on military trial for treason and breach of their oath of office. If the FPF stands in our way they will be run over.

"General McNab will be acting President along with the Chief Justice of the Supreme Court. New elections will be held as soon as possible. First however, we must get this crime and terrorism under control, thereby restoring law and order. It's a big job but some states like Utah, Arizona, Texas and Montana are already under control. We have new enlistments joining our forces every day. The worst places are Washington, New York, L.A., and generally the northeast and west coast. Any states that do not support this cause will have their Governors arrested and also put on trial."

Tommy asked, "How long will this take?"

The General replied, "We expect it may take up to another year. This is why your support is critical."

Rick stated, "Your Rangers and their families are more than welcome here. We stand behind you 100% and agree that the President overstepped his lawful bounds, while a spineless Congress did nothing to stop him. We need new elections. We are lucky to have you here. If you give us a list of the family names we will select proper housing for them and assign people to help them move into the compound."

The General replied, "Thank you Rick, for your comments. We feel right at home here already. Now if I may, I would like Jack, your Director of Security, and Tommy Gunn to take us on a tour around the island."

I responded, "Yes Sir, we will take two trucks; one

for all of us and one for your security team."

Captain Sessions replied, "Ok mount up. Security take the red truck, and we'll be in the blue one."

I drove with the General sitting next to me and Tommy in the back seat with the Colonel and Captain.

The General asked, "Have you had any trouble here over the last year?"

Tommy answered, "Yes Sir we have had small groups of five to ten people try to breach our island but they gave up real quick when they saw how many men we have. Our biggest skirmish happened five days ago. Captain Sessions warned us of ten cars about 60 miles away coming in our direction; they arrived here a few days later.

"There were about forty gang members at the start and we had a couple of battles with them right here at the main bridge. We eliminated about 20 of them. We aren't sure but we think some of them are hiding in the first high-rise down the road about a mile. They did manage to kill two of our people, sorry to say."

Captain Sessions asked, "Which gang are they affiliated with?"

"Captain, we don't know and we didn't ask them as we were too busy shooting. All their bodies were thrown into the shark-infested waters here. We called them fish food."

Everyone got a good laugh from that comment. The Captain had a point, as the gang name may be important. I hoped there weren't more of them coming because I knew some gangs can have several hundred members.

We pulled up to the bridge and everyone climbed

out of the trucks. We had ten guards posted on duty. Everyone watched as the General walked with us over the bridge and surveyed the area.

General Harper said, "We are going to put one Abrams Tank at the foot of the bridge and two Bradley fighting vehicles with four guards 24-7 as soon as they arrive in a few days. Then your security problems are over. As far as any group that may still be in that building I will have my Rangers remove them. Colonel, please take care of that."

Colonel Turner replied, "Yes Sir General, right away Sir."

Turner was on his satellite phone talking to someone in less than a minute.

I told the General, "Your security is appreciated. As for the gang, we are not sure they are all bad, some may be held against their will and some are women. We managed to save four little kids and one woman, who were being held as slaves. They tried to sell them to us."

Harper said, "Slaves, my God! This country has gone to hell!"

Then I told them the story about little Shanda coming to us and the bomb in her backpack. The Colonel got on his phone immediately and in 15 minutes a Black Hawk flew overhead and landed in the road.

Out jumped one Ranger who said, "Master Sergeant Smith, reporting as ordered."

"Jack, can you take Master Sergeant Smith to where the bomb bag is located? He will inspect and disarm it on the spot," ordered Colonel Turner.

I replied, "Ok, Master Sergeant, let's go." As we walked down the road the chopper took off, blowing dust in our faces while we held on to our hats.

We reached the spot where I sank the bomb and I told Smith there was a radio wired up to it. He pulled the bag to the surface of the water, peeked inside for a minute, and retrieved the radio.

Smith said, "Nothing to worry about; the radio is dead from the saltwater and it is not wired. The dynamite is real however."

That meant my theory about Shanda's mother was correct. She was not a dirt bag who wanted to murder everyone, including her daughter.

Going back to the bridge, I asked the Colonel, "When your men go into the building can you have them look for a woman named Shanda, and have her brought here, so she can be reunited with her daughter?"

Turner affirmed, "Roger that, on with the tour."

On our way to the bridge at NO MAN'S LAND a little sign on the side of the road that had been there for years read BURIAL MOUND of the TOCABAGA Indians.

The General said, "Interesting, I will name this island compound CAMP TOCABAGA in honor of the original inhabitants, the Indians, and NO MAN'S LAND is Fort DeSoto, the original 1898 name of this fort.

"Jack, do you have an email address?"

I replied, "No, I don't now but I used to have one a few years ago. The internet doesn't work well anymore."

"I suggest you set up an email address that you can use to communicate with me and others. How does tocabaga.jack sound to you? It is easy to remember. You can tap into our Army wireless email system. Captain Sessions will set up your own Army Gmail account and issue you a new super smart phone."

"Thank you, that sounds good to me. We may need to keep in contact."

"Yes we will Jack, as my wife and little boy will be coming here to live and I am making you my primary contact. I'll be counting on you to watch out for them since you are Director of Security here. I would like you to notify me if any problems arise."

"No problem, General, I will watch them as I do my own family, so no need to worry. I will arrange some housing close to mine and provide your wife with whatever she may need."

"Thank you Jack I know I can count on you and the good people living here. It is a great relief to know they will be safe."

Pulling up to the bridge to NO MAN'S LAND the General said, "I have eighty men now securing Fort Desoto and getting it ready for the rest of the Rangers. Please have these cars moved out of the way. Also, move the cars at the main bridge when our convoy shows up."

I asked Tommy, "Can you make sure that is done?"

Tommy replied, "Yes Sir, no problem."

Tommy had the cars moved to the side of the road.

I told the Colonel and Captain, "Your Rangers can make use of these cars if they need them for patrols. The keys are in the ignition. This channel is called the shark channel. It is full of sharks and fast-moving water. If anyone tries to breach the island this is a weak point that should be guarded. We had one man killed here when the gang tried to land here the other day."

Captain Sessions replied, "I understand and will place two men here 24-7 as this is the entrance to the Fort. That takes care of the north and south bridges. What about the east and west side of the island?"

I informed him, "We put four men on each side. If you'd like, we can still cover that or we can show you the locations we use for the best views."

Captain Sessions commented, "We will cover that also in the future. Please have one of your men show Master Sergeant Smith the locations."

I got on the radio and called Eddy, asking him to show Sergeant Smith the east and west side security points.

We jumped back into the trucks and drove into NO MAN'S LAND.

I told them, "Please note we are farming this land and it helps feed our compound. The gardens are outlined with white string on sticks. Our people come here almost every day to tend the crops."

We pulled up to the old fort built in 1898, now the headquarters, set up by the Rangers. Colonel Turner told Captain Sessions to warn the men not to destroy the gardens. Lucky for us the Black Hawks did not land in the fields but in the roadway.

Satisfied that his men were progressing well at Fort Desoto the General said, "Let's go back to town."

I asked the General, "How about some grilled fish and fruit for lunch?"

"That sounds great, Jack," replied General Harper.

We loaded into the trucks and headed downtown to the bar.

The General asked me, "How do you feed everyone?"

"All most everyone provides for their own family. But we have community fishermen, hunters and farmers who mass-produce what we eat. It is brought to our three restaurants to divide up. Anyone can choose their portion between the hours of 7am to 9pm. We have a goal of 500 pounds of fish a day and whatever rabbits or squirrels are killed over in NO MAN'S LAND, excuse me, I mean Fort Desoto. In addition, we have a chicken farm here supplying eggs and sometimes the whole chicken. It is just down the road about a half mile. The chicken farmer lives there."

General Harper asked me, "Can you increase the food supply and also provide my Rangers meat and vegetables?"

"Absolutely, we just need to plant more crops and increase the number of men we have fishing and hunting, and since we will not have as many men on security, it should be easy. I will discuss the details with Captain Sessions."

The Colonel replied, "We cannot have hunters walking around the Fort area with guns near our Rangers as someone could get hurt. So hunting with a gun is out, you need to use traps. As a matter of fact, no one can enter the Fort without a pass. We will issue everyone an ID badge on Camp Tocagaba, to avoid an accident. I will have the badges ready in about a week; they'll only have a number on them with no pictures or names. You can add the names and pictures later."

"Great Colonel, when they are ready let me know. I'll give you a list for your reference. I suggest you have about 1,000 printed up."

"That sounds perfect, Jack."

We all agreed as security was the number one concern.

Colonel Turner asked, "How many men do you have on security detail?"

I advised him, "We have a total of 96 trained men and women on our security teams. Each team has sixteen people on every shift, around the clock."

"To make this easy keep your security teams as they are for now. We will keep two Rangers at the bridge to the Fort and assign four Rangers at the main bridge along with two Bradleys and the Abrams when they arrive. That should suffice for now and we will sort it out further when our main force arrives."

Returning downtown, we walked into the bar and Tony asked, "What would you gentlemen like?"

General Harper replied, "Son, give us some cold beers. "

"Well Sir I have cool beers but not cold ones. We have no ice."

I said, "General Harper, this is Tony. If you need anything done right he is the go-to guy. Tony, this is General Harper the man in charge of the Rangers so treat him well."

Tony responded, "It is a pleasure to meet you Sir. We are happy you're here."

"Good to meet you Tony. Cool or cold, I'll take a beer and we will arrange for you to have ice in the future."

I asked, "Tony can we get some smoked fish and a variety of fruit brought in so we can have lunch with the General?"

Without another word Tony was on the radio and asked Steve, the best cook we have, to please bring lunch to the bar for five VIP people.

Tony has been the barkeep forever and is a handy guy to have around. He went to med school but dropped out in his fourth year, so he knows more about medical issues than most people. Steve is a great cook and expert in preparing fish; he has been a cook for thirty years. Steve loves to cook for people and all you need to do is bring him the fish or whatever you want to eat and he turns it into a delicious dish. He makes a pretty mean rabbit and rattlesnake stew.

After lunch the Colonel said, "General Sir, I received a message that a troop of 100 Federal Police with armored trucks is heading in this direction. I think they will make Camp Tocabaga a target. They're about two days away so I suggest we move the Abrams and two Bradleys here now from Tampa along with 100 Rangers. We need to protect this camp and fort."

The General replied, "Ok Colonel, make it so. Double-time it; I want the armor here tomorrow. Do the Feds have any air support?"

"General, I believe they do, but we are not sure at this time."

General Harper stated, "The Colonel is in command now, I need to go to SOCOM and make sure my Rangers and Armor arrive soon. Remember, if the Feds show up give them a chance to surrender but take no risks. If any Federal officers surrender take their fingerprints, DNA and pictures. They must sign a pledge not to enforce Executive Order 13603 or fight the Military. We will let them go home or they can enlist in the Army and join our side. In any case, Colonel Turner contact me if any situations arise. I bid you all a good day and thank you for lunch."

We said farewell to the General as Sessions and Turner saluted him. He returned a salute and the General with his security team mounted up in the Black Hawk. The motors wound up, the blades screaming louder and louder, and it lifted off in a blast of wind and noise.

Sessions said, "I'll have four Rangers posted at the main bridge and two at the Fort bridge within the hour, so please advise your security people."

Tommy radioed everyone to inform them of this with the click of a button.

Captain Sessions and Colonel Turner advised us they must leave to oversee the security and plans for the new Rangers coming. We all shook hands and Sessions gave me his military radio to contact him if anything developed tonight. Jumping in their Black Hawk, they lifted off and flew to the Fort for the night.

I was thinking, *I sure hope the 100 extra Rangers get here with the tanks before the Federal Police arrive.*

April 24, 2025

Early the next day two Bradley fighting vehicles and one Abrams tank rumbled up to the bridge. Captain Sessions must have been at the bridge before daylight. He was giving the Bradley and Tank operators their positions while we moved our cars to the south of the bridge on the side of the road, out of the way, keeping them there for future use if needed.

Along with the tanks were thirty trucks loaded with 100 Rangers and supplies. The trucks rolled over the old bridge and it creaked from their weight. I knew the Abrams tank could never cross the bridge because it weighed too much; the bridge could collapse.

As the trucks rolled down the street people lined up, cheered, waved, threw flowers and shouted, "Welcome Rangers, thanks for coming!"

The Rangers were surprised by the welcome. The trucks continued past our downtown area on to NO MAN'S LAND. They had orders to set up camp, which meant housing, cooking areas, a mess hall, shower areas, latrines, and so forth. They had a lot of work to do.

Sessions placed the two Bradleys on each side of the road at the foot of the bridge and put the Abrams tank right in the middle of the road. The tank was so wide it just about covered the two ten-foot wide lanes. No car could get by the 60-ton tank. These are the biggest bad-ass fighting machines ever made. After the vehicles were in position Sessions, Tommy and I walked down to get a closer look at these incredible machines. The tank had a name painted on its side, "Iron Maiden." As we looked at it the top hatch opened up and to my surprise out popped a woman's head.

Sessions asked her, "Did you encounter any gun fire on the way here, Captain?"

She replied, "No Sir, who would be nuts enough to fire at us?"

Sessions then announced, "Jack, this is Captain Riley the tank commander. Captain, this is Jack Gunn Director of Security for Camp Tocabaga, and his son, Tommy Gunn."

I said, "Captain, it is a pleasure to meet you. I like the name of your tank."

She responded, "The pleasure is mine Sir. We are here to help protect Camp Tocabaga and Fort Desoto and we will not let you down."

Tommy replied, "You've got a big gun for a woman, but I like it. Welcome to Camp Tocabaga."

Captain Riley gave no reply to Tommy's comment.

Captain Sessions took us over to each Bradley and introduced the commanders. The Bradleys are commanded by a Staff Sergeant or higher and operate as a unit along with the Abrams Tank. They are under the overall command of the Tank Captain. Each Bradley can hold six fully armed Rangers.

One Bradley was named "Predator," and the other "Gun Smoke."

The Bradley M3 Fighting Vehicle, named after General Omar Bradley from WWII, has a three-member crew, weighs 27 tons and is fully armored. It fires a 25mm chain gun that can destroy most tanks and has a 7.62 M240 machine gun to mow down ground troops if needed. Some also have tow missiles that can blow up anything, even a building.

The M1 Abrams Tank named after General Abrams, fires a whopping 120mm laser-aimed cannon and never misses its target. The cannon can blow up buildings. It has one M2 50 Caliber Heavy Machine Gun, and two 7.62 M240 machine guns. Bullets and other large projectiles just bounce off the sides of this big boy. Now we were talking real security!

Colonel Turner and Captain Sessions asked Tommy and me, along with the armored-vehicle commanders, to meet to discuss clearing the building where the gang was located. We sat under the bridge in the shade and I drew them a picture in the dirt of the building layout, parking area and the main entrance to the building. I briefed them on the weapons the gang may have and the fact that they may have some explosives.

I told everyone that I thought they were on the top floor of the ten-story building. Each floor has four condo units. I advised them we were looking for a woman named Shanda. We didn't have her description but there couldn't be too many women there. I added that she may be dangerous but we didn't know for sure.

The beautiful Captain Riley asked, "Tommy, would you come along and help search for this Shanda while the Rangers are doing security and room clearing as necessary?"

"I would be pleased to go with you, Captain Riley," Tommy replied.

"Great, we will have 11 Rangers, the two Bradleys and the tank will go for extra support. Let's be ready to roll out at 15:00 hours," Sessions ordered. "If nothing else, you are all dismissed."

Tommy hung around after the meeting talking to Captain Riley, much to my dismay. Tommy doesn't need to mess around as he has a great wife and little girl. I thought, *I will chew his ass out later.*

It was another hot day; as I drove to the bridge, it was almost 15:00 hours or 3 pm standard eastern time. I watched as the Rangers and Tommy mounted up in the Bradleys. They went down the road one at a time with the tank last. Spaced about 100 feet apart, moving about 10 mph, it would take them about ten minutes to reach the building.

Soon you could hear rifle fire and the Bradley 25 mm rapid fire chain gun. From our position on the bridge we could only see smoke but we did listen to the radio. Gun Smoke, Predator, and Iron Maiden surrounded the building, the Rangers dismounted, and in rapid order they entered it. We heard small arms fire; they had to run up ten floors, clearing four condos on each floor to ensure it was safe to move up.

We heard on the radio a request for the Abrams tank to fire into the top floor west side of the building. We heard a large... KABOOM, which meant the big 120mm cannon had been fired. After about two hours we heard on the radio the building was clear for Tommy Gunn to come in.

Thirty minutes later Tommy radioed us, "We have no one alive, sorry to say. They were all killed in the clearing. We found one woman on the tenth floor and she has an ID card stating her name is Shanda Jones. She was shot in the head but not by us. It looks like she has been dead for a while."

I thought, *Don't mess with the Rangers. They just killed everyone in the building, and good or bad they are all dead.*

Tommy brought back the ID card which had a picture on it and gave it to Amy. Amy showed little Shanda the picture ID and asked, "Is this your Mommy?"

She replied, "Yes! Where is she?"

We were all silent.

"Shanda, honey, your Mommy and Daddy have gone to heaven. You know what heaven is?"

"Yes, I had a puppy that went to heaven."

Amy replied, "Yes, that's right. So don't worry; this is your home now and we will be your new family."

Little Shanda said, "Good I like it here. Do I call you Mommy now?"

"Yes, if you like, call me Mommy."

She hugged and kissed Amy on the cheek, then little Shanda went outside, jumped on the red bike I gave her and pedaled away.

Amy yelled, "Don't go far. Stay close to home!"

Shanda called back, "OK, Mommy!"

It seemed little Shanda did not fully understand

what had happened to her mother and father. At that age, who does? Little Shanda was going to be fine as now she had clean clothes, meals, toys, family, and a nice home to live in where she could sleep in the safety of her own bedroom. She was better off here with us.

Maybe one day she will call me Grandpa.

APRIL 25, 2025

Captain Sessions called me on the radio and advised that the Federal Police were on the way. His small drone planes had spotted them approaching about ten miles away. He said he had his Rangers building defensive positions on both sides of the bridge and wanted me to come up to the bridge with Tommy and review the defensive lines.

Colonel Turner had 100 Rangers moved up from Fort Desoto, or NO MAN'S LAND, to the bridge, all armed to the teeth and ready for action. Captain Sessions arranged the two Bradleys, one each on the east and west side of the road, and the Iron Maiden in the middle of the road at the start of the bridge, so no vehicle would be able to pass. Alongside of the vehicles sand bags were stacked and 50 caliber machine guns were placed at the far ends to allow for a cross fire pattern.

Captain Sessions asked Tommy, "Can you set up a sniper position on the top of the high and dry boat building? It is about 50 feet high and should give you a good view."

Tommy said, "Great, I will get the Cobb 50 and the 308 rifle up there ASAP. Dad can be my spotter."

"Good idea," I replied.

Sessions told us not to shoot until he gave the order over the radio. This defensive spot on the building with the Cobb 50 would allow us to kill anyone within 1000 yards. The enemy would have no place to hide on the narrow roadway; it could be a blood bath. I wouldn't want to be in their shoes when the shooting started.

Tommy and I quickly scrambled up the ladder to the top of the 50-foot roof of the high and dry building. We asked some Rangers to help us bring up about 20 sand bags for protection and as a shooting platform. We piled the sand bags about two high in one row, leaving a small open space for us to place our rifles, acting as a shooting window. We would be lying on the roof so we needed blankets put down because the roof was so hot.

When we were ready Tommy radioed to Captain Session, "Captain Sir we are all set on the rooftop."

Sessions answered, "Ok remember; do not fire until I give you the order to do so. Also, from now on maintain radio silence as the enemy may be listening."

"Yes Sir I copy," Tommy replied.

I admit I was nervous but also confident that we could defeat 100 Feds with our Rangers and defensive positions. Still I did not want anyone to be killed or hurt in the exchange. Once the shooting starts you are not nervous or worried, you become focused only on killing the enemy.

That's what it was like a few days ago fighting the gang at the bridges. We didn't have the full force of the Rangers then and I was worried. I must admit, I was also a little scared until the shooting started. Of course I fired the first shot, but once I decided to kill Big Jim, I was ready to do it. My countless hours of training, shooting and practice made me positive I would win a gun battle against any untrained puss bags.

As Tommy and I lay on the roof I told him, "Son, I

am proud of you."

"Thanks Dad you taught me everything I know. I remember the first time you took me shooting when I was ten years old. That was a thrill."

"I've noticed little Shanda and Kendra are playing together a lot. I think Shanda is going to be fine. She also knows the kids who where slaves so they all are friends and spend time together."

Kendra is my ten-year-old granddaughter and I would give my life for her. At least now Kendra could play with kids her age.

"Tommy, I'd bet a lot of little kids out there need help, need a home and food. I am going to make that my mission, to search for them all over the city, when things calm down, and bring them here."

"That sounds good count me in on that."

Our conversation was interrupted when Ron, Robbie and Eddy showed up on the roof. They brought us water and a snack. It was now 11 am and the sun was getting hot. I wanted off of the hot roof as we had no shade.

Robbie asked me, "What can I do to help? I need to do something; the Rangers don't want any of us near the front line."

Robbie thought he was invincible and nothing could hurt him. That kind of thinking will get you killed, sooner or later.

I told everyone, "Just sit here and watch. We are the last defense if the Feds break our lines then we have to go down and back-up the Rangers. Tommy and I will be shooting from here if Sessions gives us the order. We have all put our lives on the line many times. Let's not get killed now that the situation is improving."

As we were waiting and watching suddenly Gun Smoke and about 50 men started to quickly move down the road toward the building that we cleared. I wondered what Turner and Sessions had up their sleeves.

Robbie asked, "What the hell are they doing?"

I replied, "I don't know but it seems to me they are going to spring a trap on the Feds."

Then it occurred to me that they were going to hide a force in or around the buildings and once the Feds passed them, they would be sandwiched between the two Ranger forces.

I said to everyone, "Yeah, that's it. Sessions is setting a trap."

Robbie announced, "I am going down there to see what is going on."

About two more hours went by and the heat on the roof was overcoming us. We needed to find shade, so we went down the ladder and sat in the shadow of the building, leaving our sniper rifles on the roof.

Eddie said, "I am going to find Robbie. I'll be back soon. Ron you want to come along?"

"No thanks Eddy. I'll stay here with my Bro."

About two hours later we could hear the Feds coming down the road before we saw them. We scrambled back up the ladder to our positions. A scout motorcycle came zooming down the road and stopped about 600 yards from the tanks. The officer just sat there in the middle of the road looking through his binoculars. He was scouting us out to see what we had.

He looked right at us as I was looking at him through my rifle scope. We were spotted. Part of being a good sniper is not being spotted, that is a number one no-no.

Tommy said, "We need to change our location now that they've seen us. If they get closer and fire a 50-cal. machine gun at us we're toast."

I replied, "I agree, but where are we going to go?"

"Let's move to the top floor of the condos on the other side of the road. I think we would have just as good a view, maybe even better."

"Ok, let's go now before the shooting starts."

Grabbing our gear we left the rooftop, found Captain Sessions, and told him the problem and what we were doing. He agreed with us. Tommy was right the view was better but the distance set us back another 50 yards meaning we could not shoot as far. We set up on the fourth floor in an empty corner room and opened the windows. At least we were out of the hot sun. I went into the bathroom, turned on the shower, and stood under it for five minutes with my all clothes on to cool off. I can't take the sun like I once did. Ron and Tommy laughed at me.

It wasn't long before the main column pulled up behind the cycle. I could see five Hummers or HMMWVs, five new Grizzly APCs or armored personnel carriers, and three big trucks. A total of thirteen vehicles.

The Hummer carries four men and a 50-cal. machine gun and also an M220 Tow missile system. They are fast and very dangerous. The Grizzly is a six-wheeled vehicle and has two 7.62 machine guns and can withstand any 50-caliber bullet. It is built for urban warfare and carries six troops. The trucks just carry men and supplies. Maybe they had a total of 120 men.

I was thinking they were not a match for the Rangers with the three tanks. If they don't surrender this would be a blood bath for sure.

The lead Hummer moved up closer, past the cycle. It was coming up to the bridge and they were holding a white flag. I was thinking, n*ot another white flag.* The Hummer stopped about 100 feet from the Bradley. The man showing himself from the roof of the vehicle was speaking into a megaphone. Next to him was a 50 caliber mounted machine gun.

"I am Captain Clinton of the Federal Police Force and we are here to enforce Presidential Executive Order 13603, which means the Government owns this property. You are hereby given notice to leave this island within 12 hours. If you do not leave we will remove you by force and you will be placed under arrest, subject to five or more years in prison."

Colonel Turner answered back using a loud speaker, "This is Colonel Turner of the United States Army, Special Forces 75th Ranger Regiment, 3rd Battalion, operating under Special Operations Command. This island is in control of the US Army and under our protection. Furthermore, we do not recognize Executive Order 13603 as a lawful order as it violates the US Constitution. We therefore are demanding you and your men surrender. Any man who surrenders must sign a pledge not to fight against the Military or enforce the Executive Order. They are free to go home or they can enlist in the Army."

Clinton blasted back, "You are not obeying the Presidential Order and you are in the military; that is treason Colonel Turner! Therefore, we must arrest you and your men. You leave me no other choice."

"Captain Clinton, evidently you have not heard what is going on. All the Special Forces of the Military have agreed not to follow order 13603 and we believe that the President is committing treason and we have a military arrest warrant out for him and his cabinet. The rest of the Military is standing down for the time being. Our other goal is to clean up the crime, gangs and terrorists, so citizens can resume living their lives. You and your Feds are running around confiscating property, guns, money and putting innocent people in jail. You violate the second amendment by taking their guns away while you let the scum roam and kill freely. Make no mistake; we will stop this and we will arrest the President and hold new elections."

There was a long pause with no reply from Captain Clinton.

"Colonel Turner I have my orders and I must insist that you surrender this island, then you, and your men can leave; I will look the other way. We have no fight with the Army Rangers. I don't know if you are telling me the truth or not."

"Captain believe me I am telling you the truth. I warn you, your small force is no match for my Rangers. We clearly have your forces out-gunned; please consider that many of your men will be killed. My Abrams tank could destroy your equipment and most of your troops with just three rounds. I must also warn you that you will not be able to leave here as you are surrounded and if you fight, it means military prison for all your men. I will give you one hour to discuss this with your men and surrender or we will open fire."

I looked at my watch; it was 2:30 pm. That meant

the deadline given by Captain Sessions was 3:30 pm.

The fifty Rangers and Gun Smoke, the Bradley fighting vehicle, came out from under cover and were now behind the Feds. They clearly had no way out. We all waited, wondering if Captain Clinton was nuts enough to attack the Ranger force. It was also clear to us that Captain Clinton was out of touch. He did not know what was going on in Washington D.C. He was a stooge for the President's private Army called the FPF or Federal Police Force, or as I call them, the men in black. Hitler also had his own private Army called the SS and they also wore black. They did all the dirty work for Hitler and they were the worst scum on earth, lower than whale droppings at the bottom of the ocean. If the FPF was anything like the SS then they all needed to die.

Rumor has it the FPF took an oath to protect and defend the President and follow his orders only. There was nothing in the oath about the Constitution. My guess is these guys have been brain-washed and if they could, they would kill us all. I hate all of them with a passion.

Time was ticking down. As I looked at my watch again I saw it was 3:15 pm; in fifteen minutes the battle would start. I had a great seat, a box seat in the shade to watch our Rangers do their job. Looking down the road I could see the Feds were lining up their vehicles across the road in two rows, five in each row. The Fed troops were in between the two rows of vehicles. All of a sudden one of their Hummers fired a missile at the Abrams. Then, all hell broke loose!

The missile hit the protective sand bags in front of the Abrams, blowing them to smithereens but also killing some of the Rangers. With the smoke and sand flying, I could not tell how many were killed. The Abrams fired the big 120 mm cannon at the Hummer that shot the missile. It promptly blew up into a big lump of burning metal.

KABOOM! Another round fired by the Iron Maiden hit another Hummer. The Bradleys were firing the 25 mm cannons in rapid succession. The Feds started firing the big machine guns and the 50-caliber bullets were flying all over the place. If one of these rounds missed their target it could fly a mile or more, so I hoped none of our people were standing too close behind the lines.

I'd told everyone in our family to stay inside when they heard the shooting start.

Sessions was on the radio to Tommy, "Take out Captain Clinton with your Cobb 50 and maybe the rest will give up before we kill them all."

Tommy replied, "Roger that, Captain."

I asked, "Tommy, can you see Clinton?"

"Yeah, he is trying to hide behind an APC, but I've got a clear shot at his head."

Tommy was taking aim. Ron and I were watching through our scopes and without warning ... KABAM! ... Tommy fired. We watched Clinton's head explode, a blood red mist went up in the air, and his body fell to the ground.

Tommy called Sessions, "Captain the target is eliminated, Sir."

"Roger that," Sessions replied.

After about five minutes the shooting tapered down and finally stopped. The Feds raised a white flag, meaning they surrendered. The men started to throw down their guns and climb out of the Hummers and APC trucks. They raised their hands and started toward the bridge. The Bradley pulled forward with its machine guns ready and the commander told the Feds to stop and line up single file. Captain Sessions walked down to meet them with about thirty Rangers. The battle had only lasted about seven minutes.

Sixty-five men had surrendered, with 48 killed. Four of the five Hummers were blown up and two APCs were destroyed. The Rangers proceeded to frisk each of the men and zip-tie their hands behind their backs. Captain Sessions told them they were all under arrest for attacking the US Army and they were enemy combatants. They were loaded up and taken to Ft. Desoto in their own trucks. The prisoners would be moved to another location far away from us in a day or two.

The battle was over but six rangers were killed and much to my surprise, so was Robbie. A Ranger Medic found Robbie lying in the grass near the bridge. He had been hit by a 50 caliber BMG round and had a hole in him the size of a soft ball. He died instantly and probably never knew what hit him.

Eddy was sitting next to Robbie when I arrived. I asked Eddy, "What happened?"

Sobbing, Eddy said, "We were looking for you guys and the stupid Feds opened fire. I hit the dirt, but Robbie kept walking and got shot by a random bullet. I can't talk about it now. I don't know how his wife Maggie is going to take this; I have to go tell her."

"I'll go with you, Eddy."

We covered his body with a blanket before placing him in the truck. Robbie would be buried at sea like everyone else who had died.

A Ranger Medic approached us and asked, "Sir would you like a body bag for your friend?"

I said, "Yes, thank you. He was my good friend Robbie." Ron and Eddy helped me zip Robbie into the black bag.

I can't write more now, maybe later I will.

GOD BLESS AMERICA, LAND OF THE FREE AND HOME OF THE BRAVE.

We are waiting for you to contact us by email to find out where Tocabaga is located. There is an email address hidden these chronicles. In case you missed it... tocabaga.jack@gmail.com.

I will reply.

Jack Gunn

THOMAS H. WARD

DRAMATIS PERSONAE

Amy – Daughter of Jack Gunn, a Nurse and sharp shooter

Big Dan – Tocabaga security guard killed by the doper gang

Carlos – Tocabaga security guard

Chris – Handy man and Tocabaga security agent

Colonel Turner – Commanding Officer of the Army Rangers based at Fort   Desoto

Captain Sessions – Combat officer, commands and controls combat operations in the field

Captain Clinton - Captain of the Federal Police Force

Captain Riley – Lady tank commander, girl friend of Captain Sessions

Deputy Matthews – Sherriff Deputy in charge of Tocabaga

Doc Scott – Tocabaga doctor

Eddy – Good Friend of Jack Gunn, brews beer and grows pot and is on the security team

General Harper – General in charge of the Rangers

Hemmi – Wife of Jack Gunn.

Joan - Wife of Ron Gunn, a Nurse.

Jim Bo – Husband to Amy and Son-in- Law of Jack.

Kendra – Granddaughter of Jack Gunn, Daughter of Tommy Gunn

Maggie – Wife of Robbie, who is in charge of the farming

Mark – One of Jacks' best friends killed by the doper gang

Robbie – Best friend of Jack Gunn, a Tocabaga security guard killed by the FPF on April 25, 2025

Ron - Brother of Jack Gunn retired Navy Veteran.

Rick – President of Tocabaga association, security team member

Sammy – Tocabaga security guard wounded by the doper gang

Steve – Jacks' neighbor and security guard

Sergeant Smith - Army Ranger assigned as security guard for Jack

Shanda – Little girl, daughter of big Jim a bad guy, killed by Jack

Tommy Gunn – Son of Jack Gunn and a retired Marine Scout Sniper.

Tonya – Wife of Tommy Gunn

Tony – Bar keeper and sharp shooter for Tocabaga security.

ABOUT THE AUTHOR

Thomas H. Ward is a best-selling author of suspense thriller fiction and nonfiction works. He is best known for his ten book series Tocabaga, and Templars Quest a three book series, Critical Incidents, and Gun Talk a nonfiction book about terrorism in the United States.

Education and Experience:

Born in Chicago in 1946 and raised in Cleveland he now resides in Tampa Florida. Ward, prior to becoming an Author, was a Metallurgical Engineer and Business Owner. He obtained an MBA in International Business. Having traveled extensively to thirteen different countries his favorite ones are China, Japan, and South Korea where he was based for a period of time. He has made 150 trips to Asian and Europe over a 20-year time period, becoming conversant in three different languages. Thomas is a student of World History and the Bible.

In his younger days, during the Cold War and Vietnam War, he was employed by a government subcontractor which required a Department of Defense (DOD) Secret Clearance and Atomic Energy Commission (AEC) Classified Clearance. Over the years he became an expert in security operations and the use of small arms.

He started writing technical manuals and business

books years ago. Thomas turned to writing fictional stories when his publisher suggested he do so. "Thomas always had great stories to tell. His experience, travels, and imagination are a bonus for a fiction writer." Ward always places in his books the following quote which he composed:

"In every truth there is non-truth, in every fiction there is non-fiction."

—Thomas H. Ward

To Contact the author:

Visit his website: www.ThomasHWardBooks.com

Or by email: thomashward46@gmail.com